GW01607759

WILD PILGRIMAGE

WILD PILGRIMAGE

A Novel in Woodcuts

LYND WARD

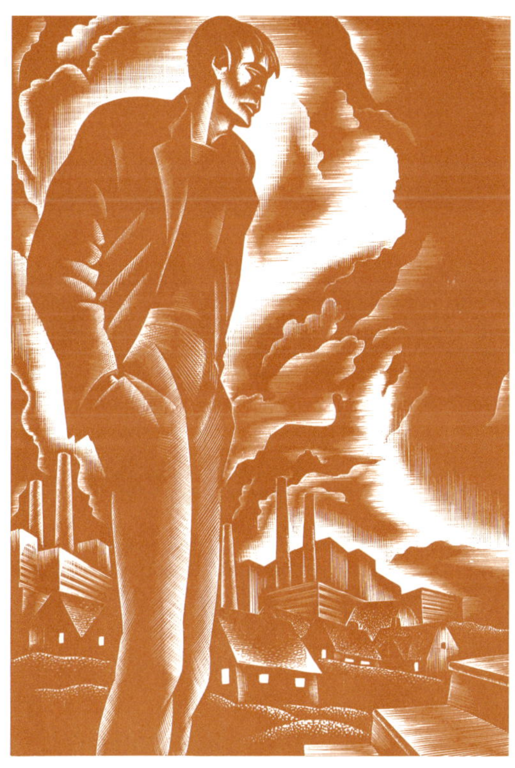

DOVER PUBLICATIONS, INC.
Mineola, New York

Copyright

Bibliographical Note

This Dover edition, first published in 2008, is an unabridged republication of the work originally published in 1932 by Harrison Smith and Robert Haas, New York. The blank pages backing up the woodcut illustrations have been eliminated for this edition.

Library of Congress Cataloging-in-Publication Data

Ward, Lynd, 1905–1985.
Wild pilgrimage : a novel in woodcuts / Lynd Ward.
p. cm.
"This Dover edition is an unabridged republication of the work originally published in 1932 by Harrison Smith and Robert Haas, New York."
ISBN-13: 978-0-486-46583-8
ISBN-10: 0-486-46583-7
1. Wood-engraving, American. I. Title.

NE1215.W3A48 2008
769.92—dc22

2007050542

Manufactured in the United States of America
Dover Publications, Inc., 31 East 2nd Street, Mineola, N.Y. 11501

TO MY FATHER
WHO SEES THESE THINGS
WITH A CLEARER EYE

...THINKING THINGS THAT CANNOT BE CHAINED AND CANNOT BE LOCKED, BUT THAT WANDER FAR AWAY IN THE SUNLIT WORLD, EACH IN A WILD PILGRIMAGE AFTER A DESTINED GOAL.

ARTURO GIOVANNITTI

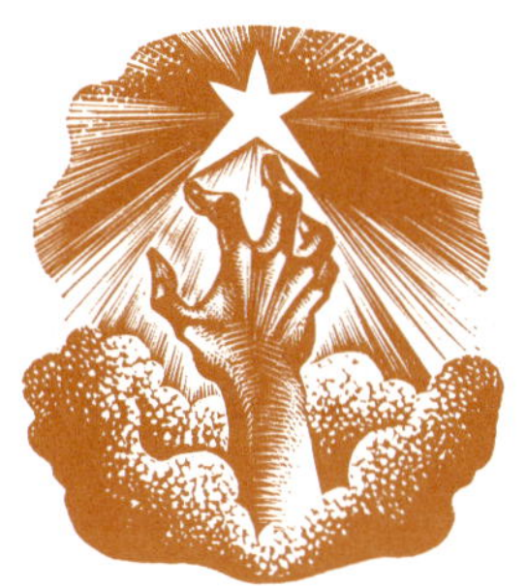

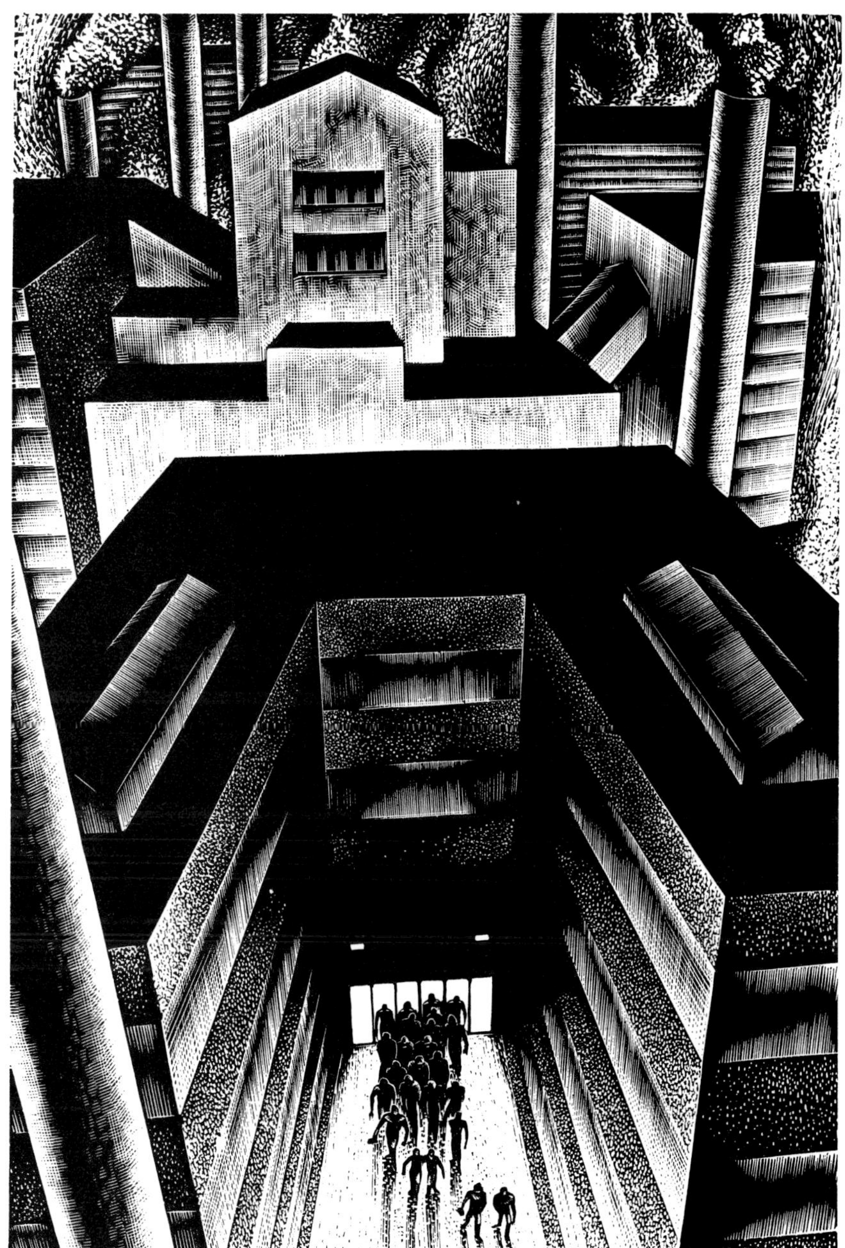

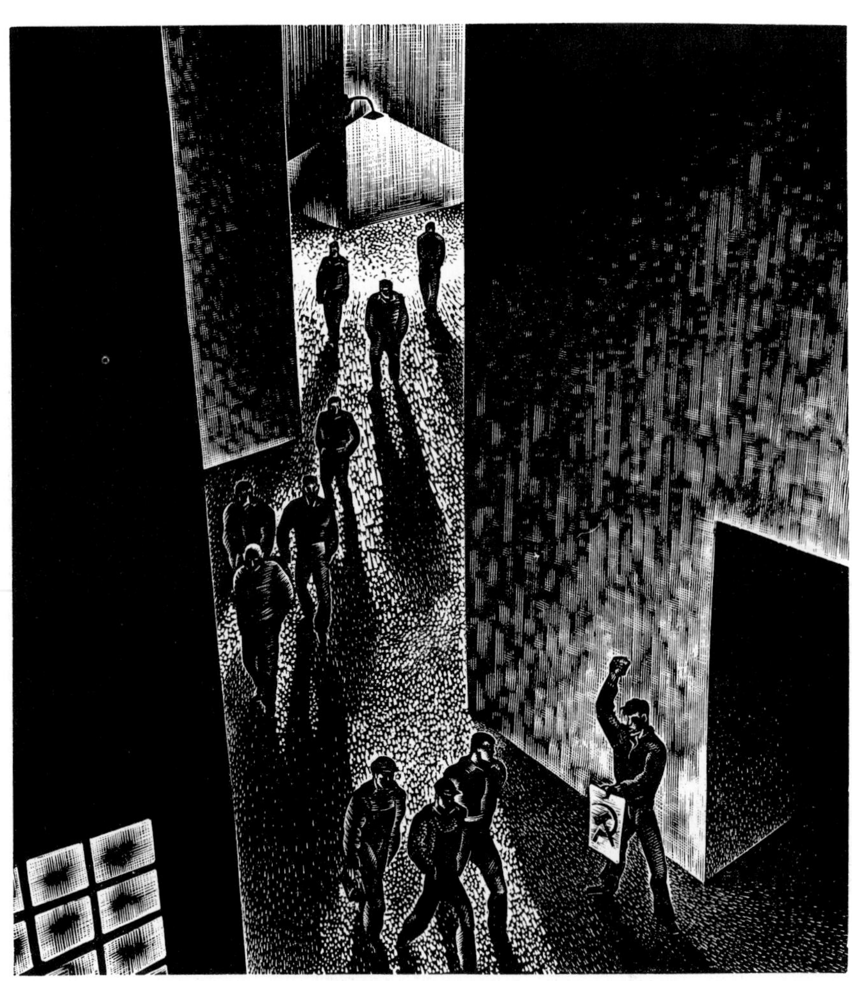

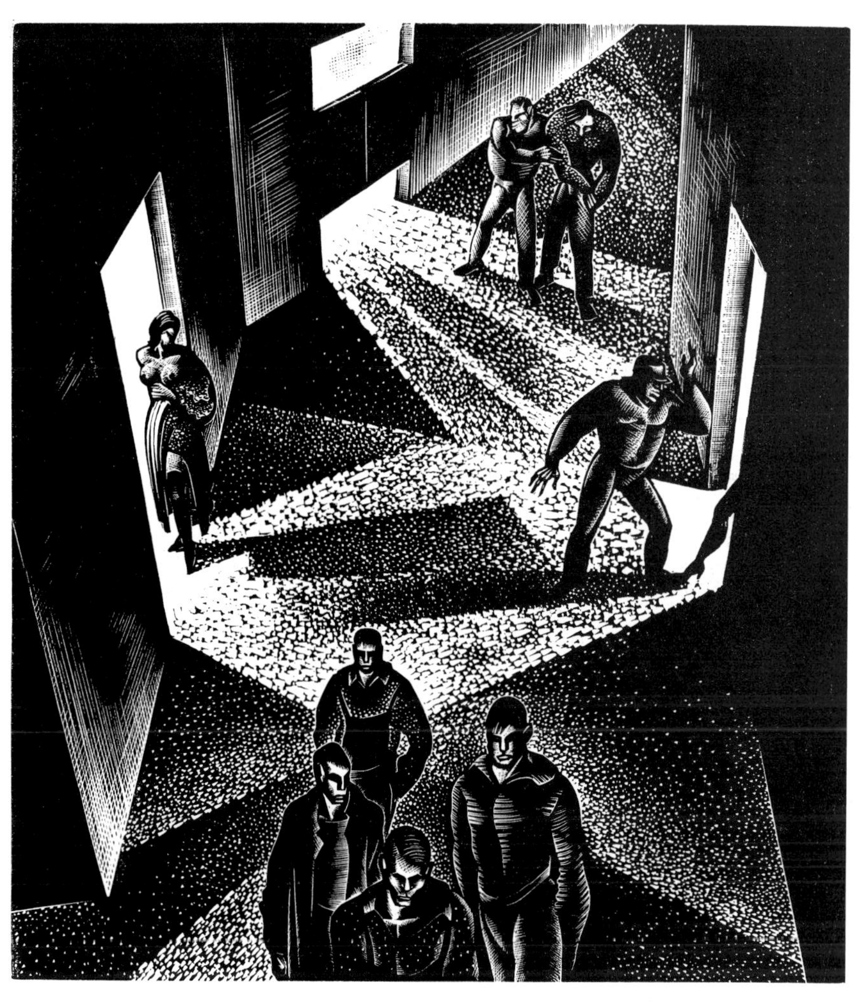

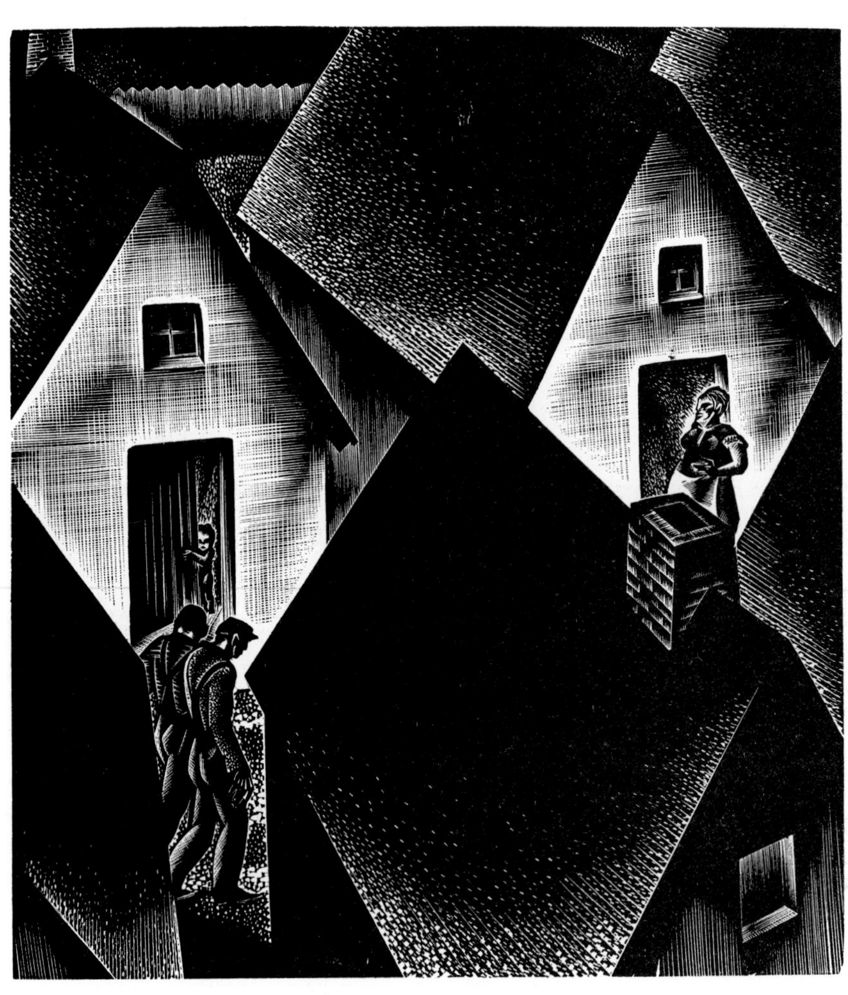

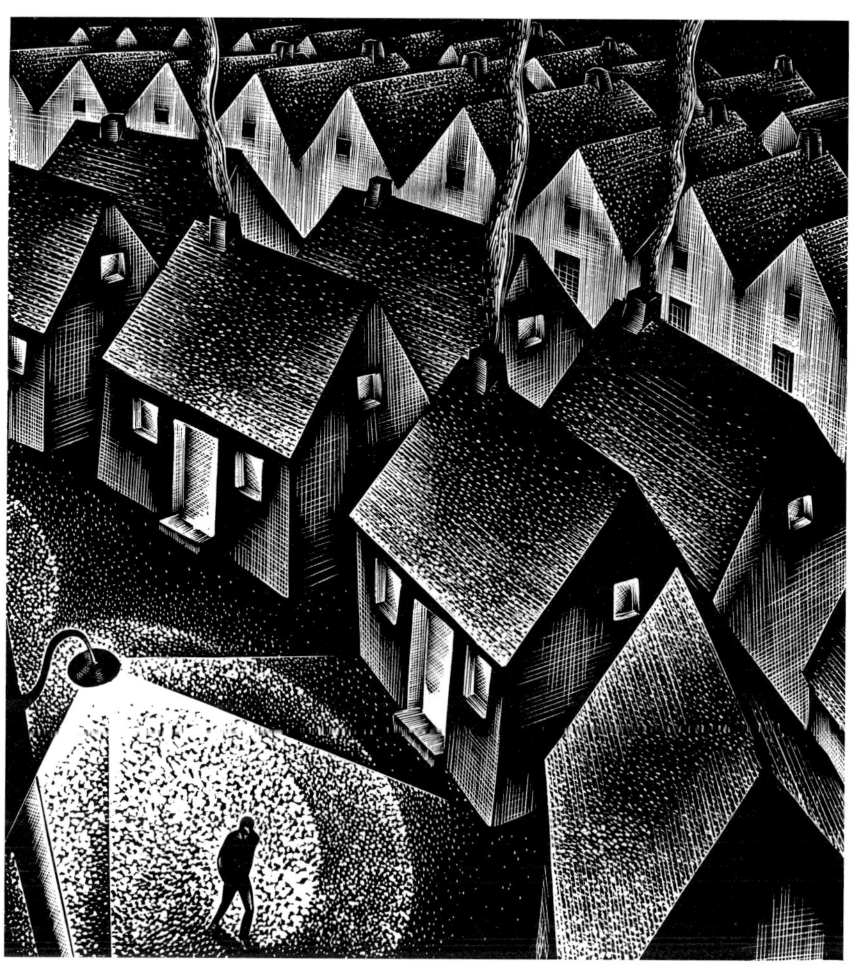

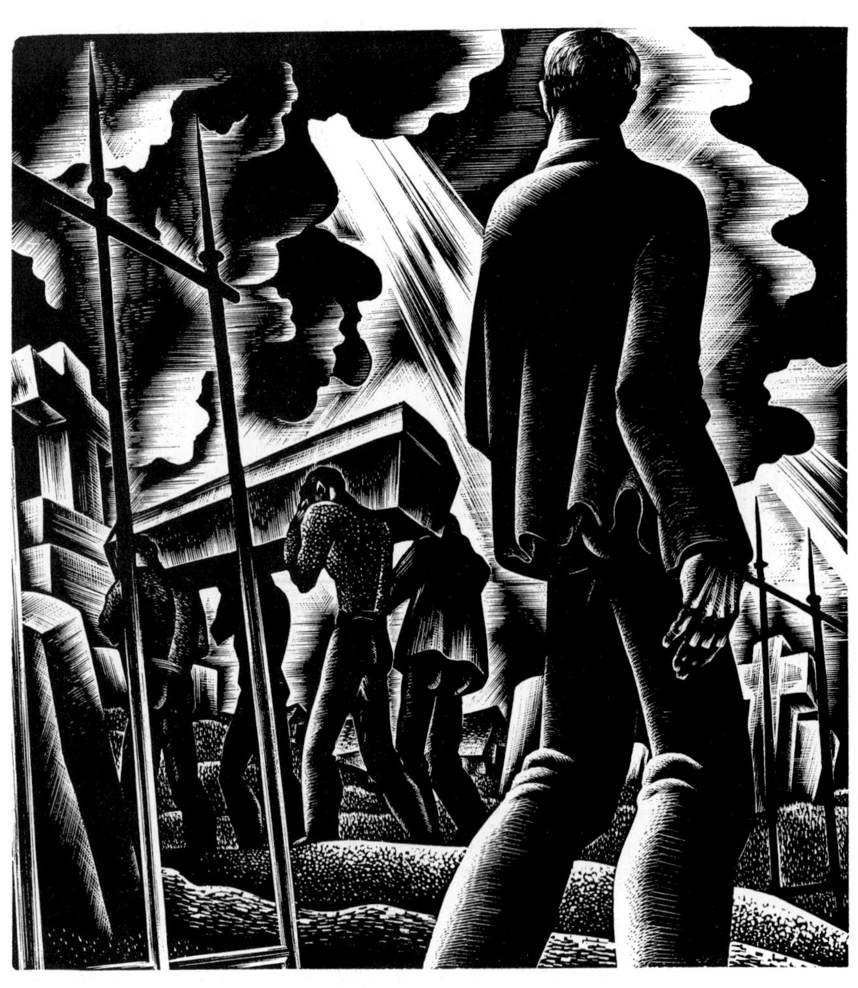

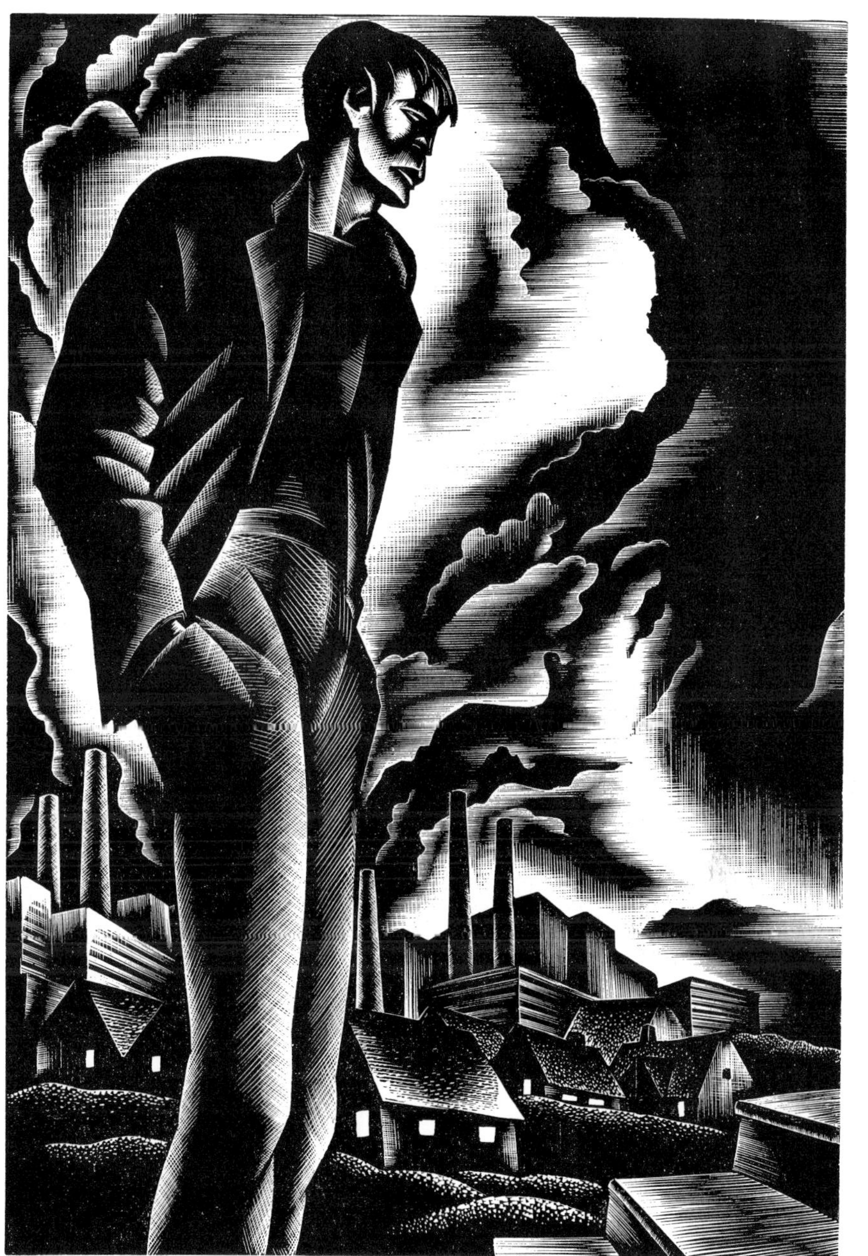

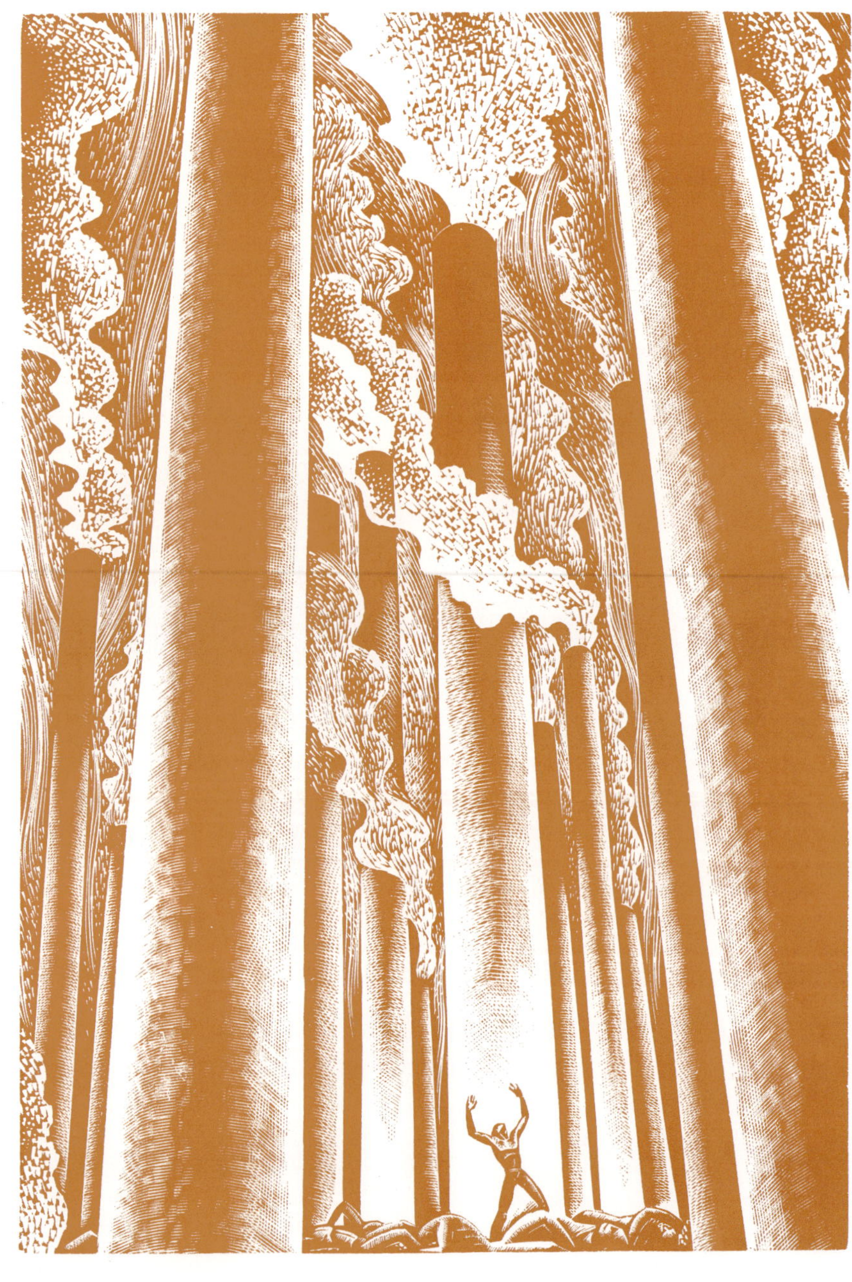

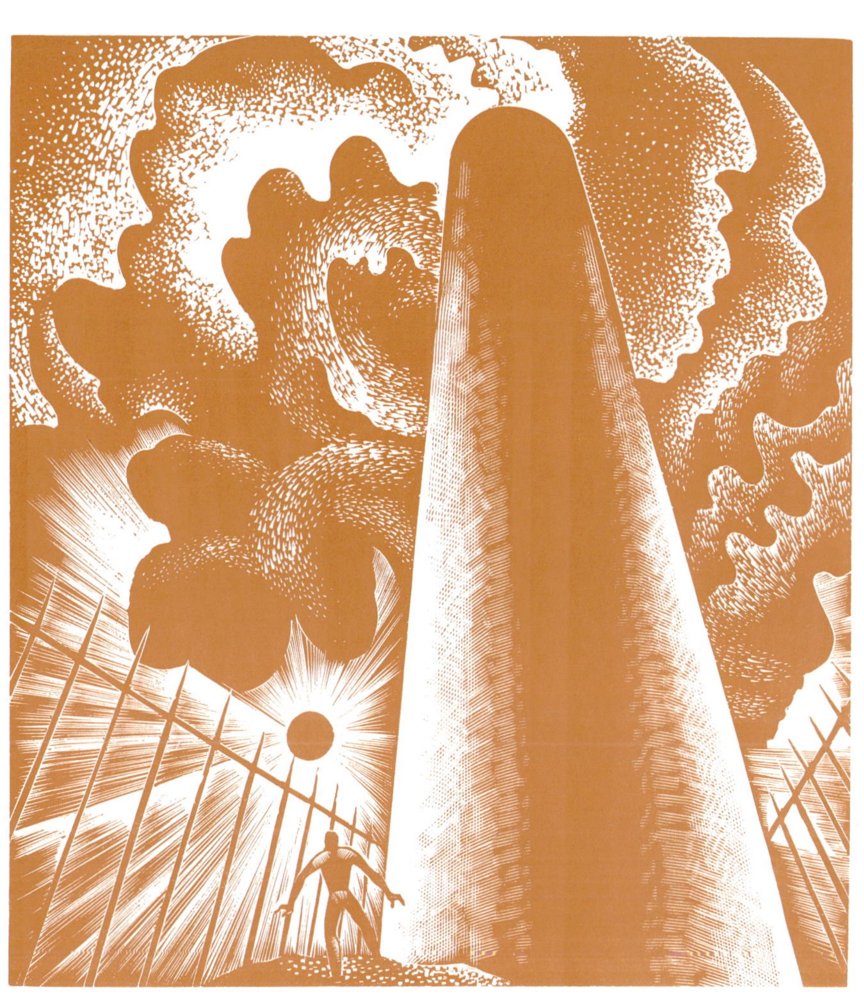

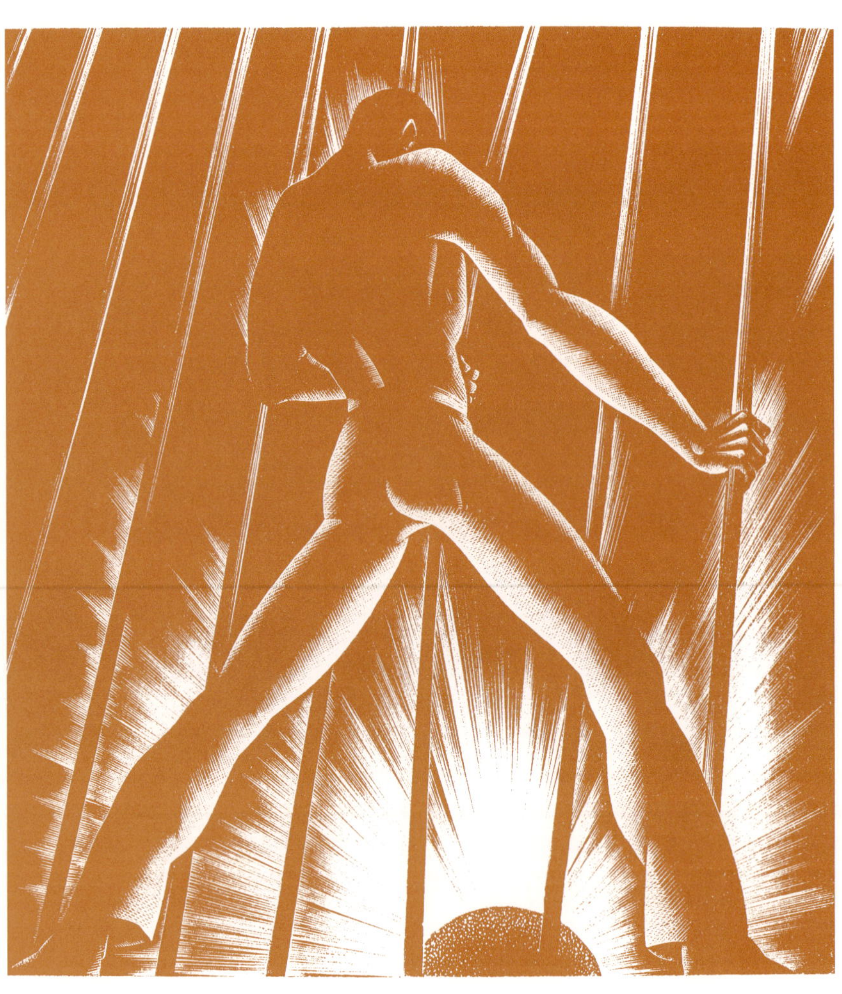

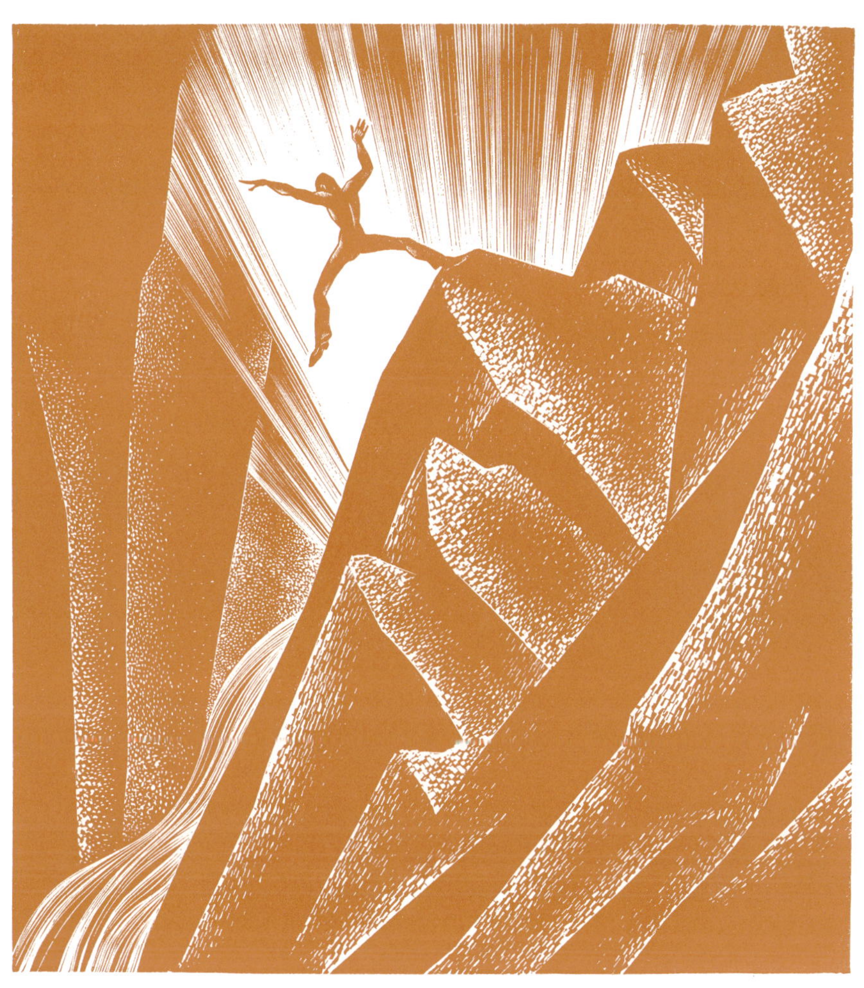

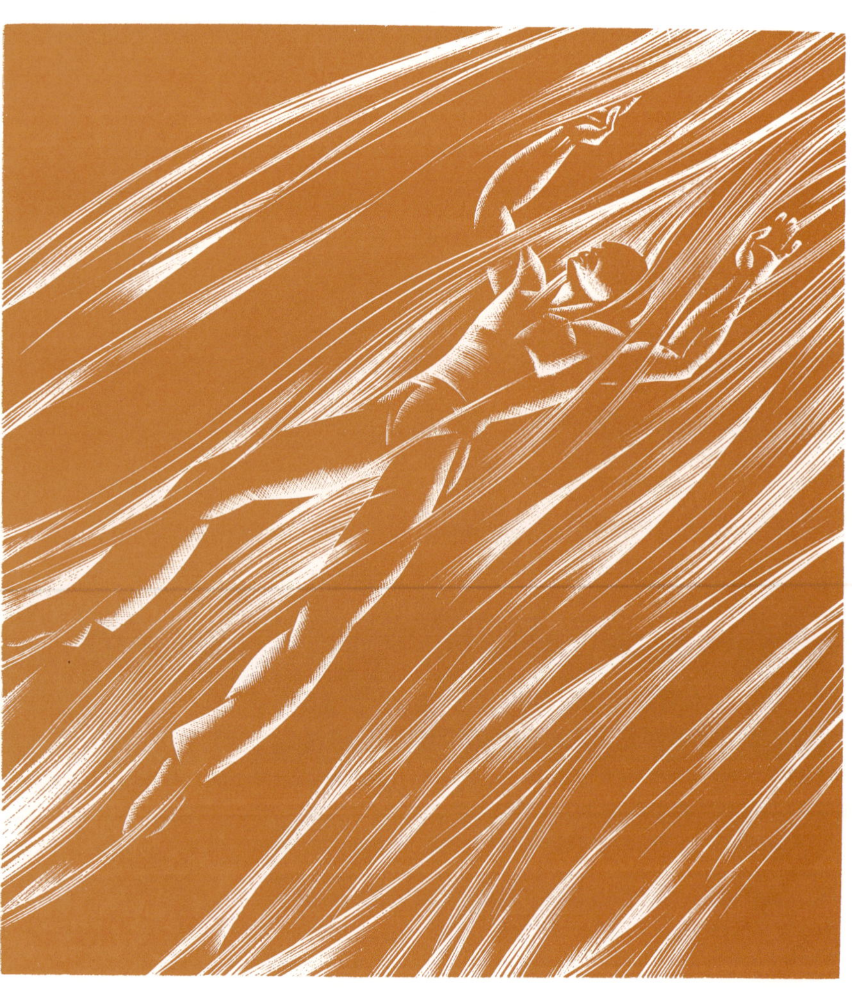

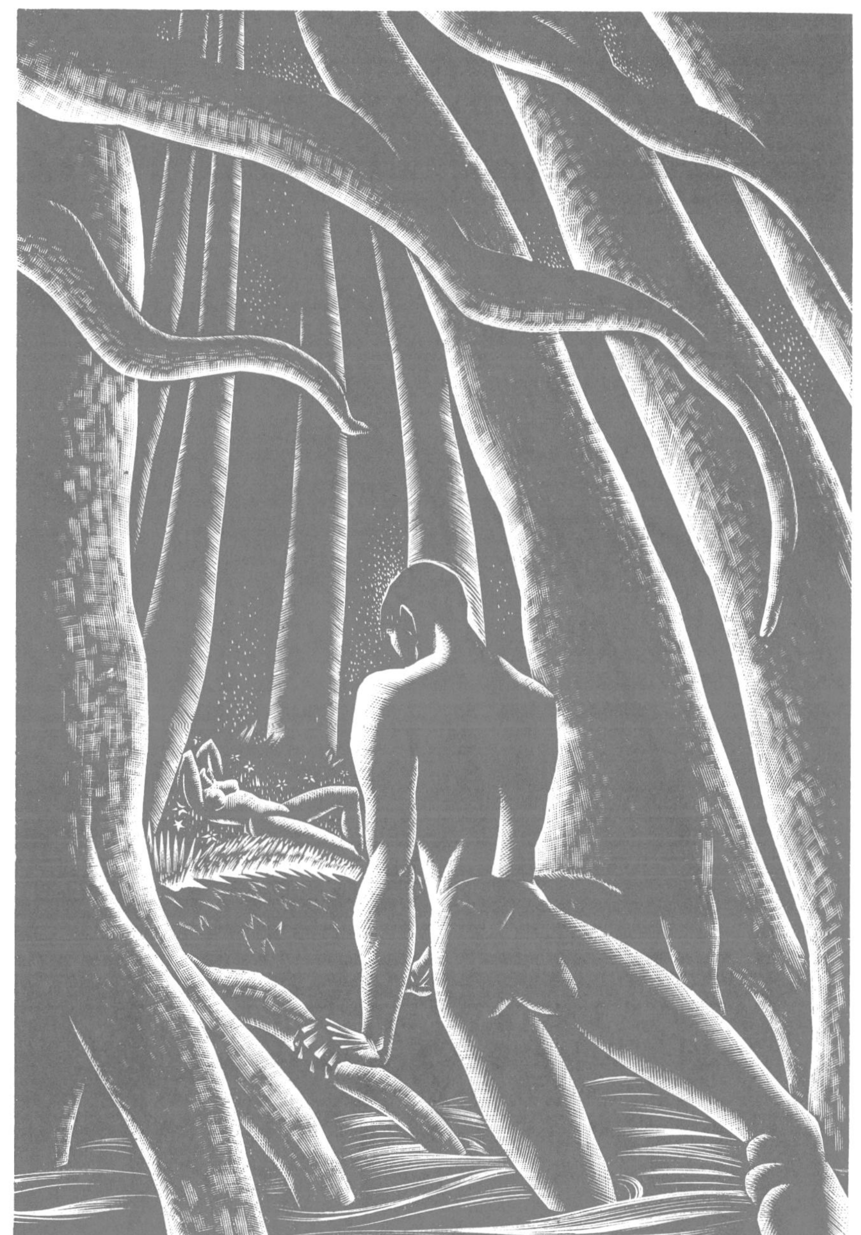

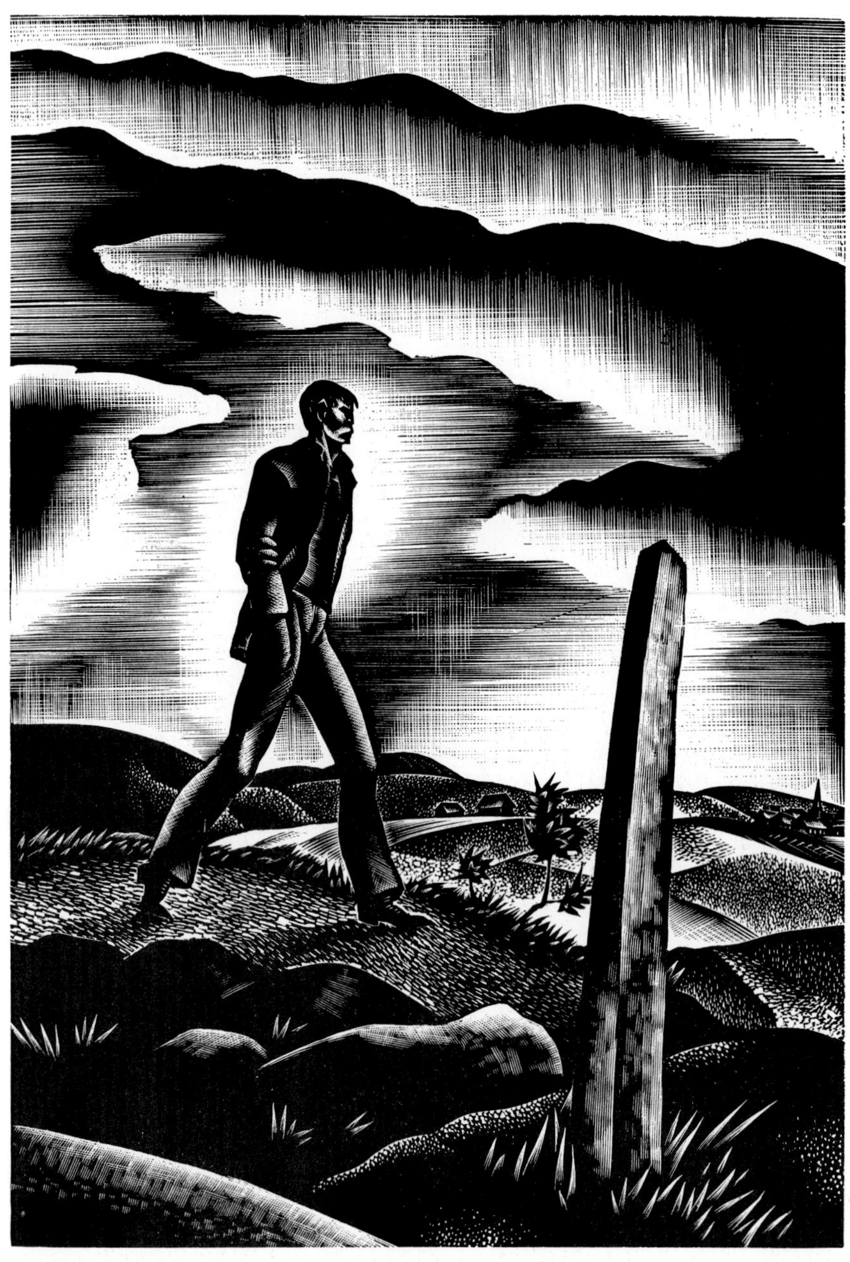

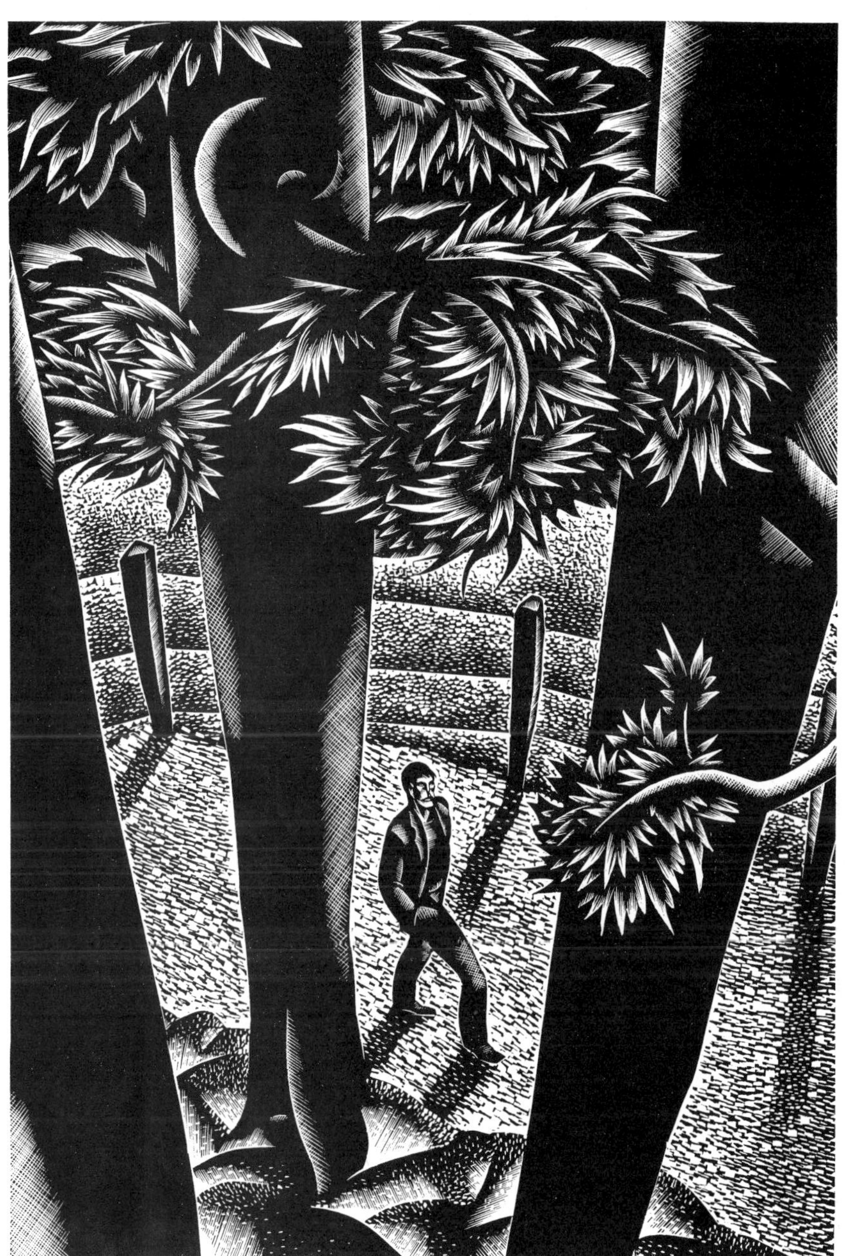

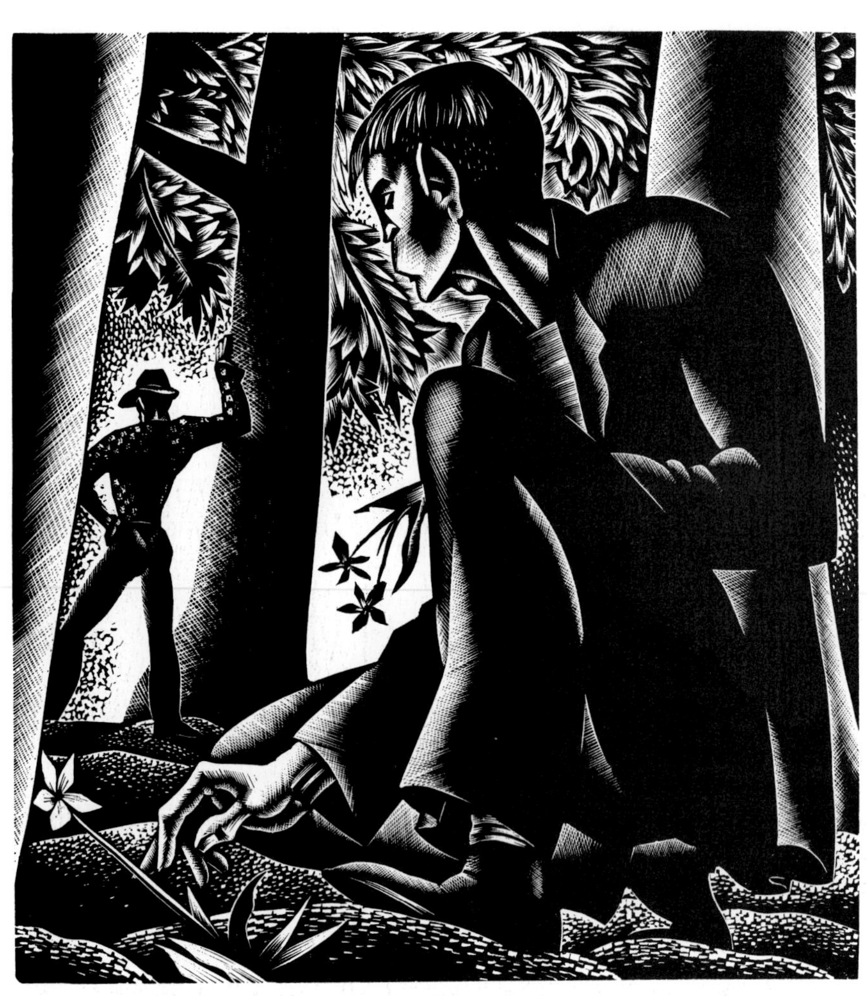

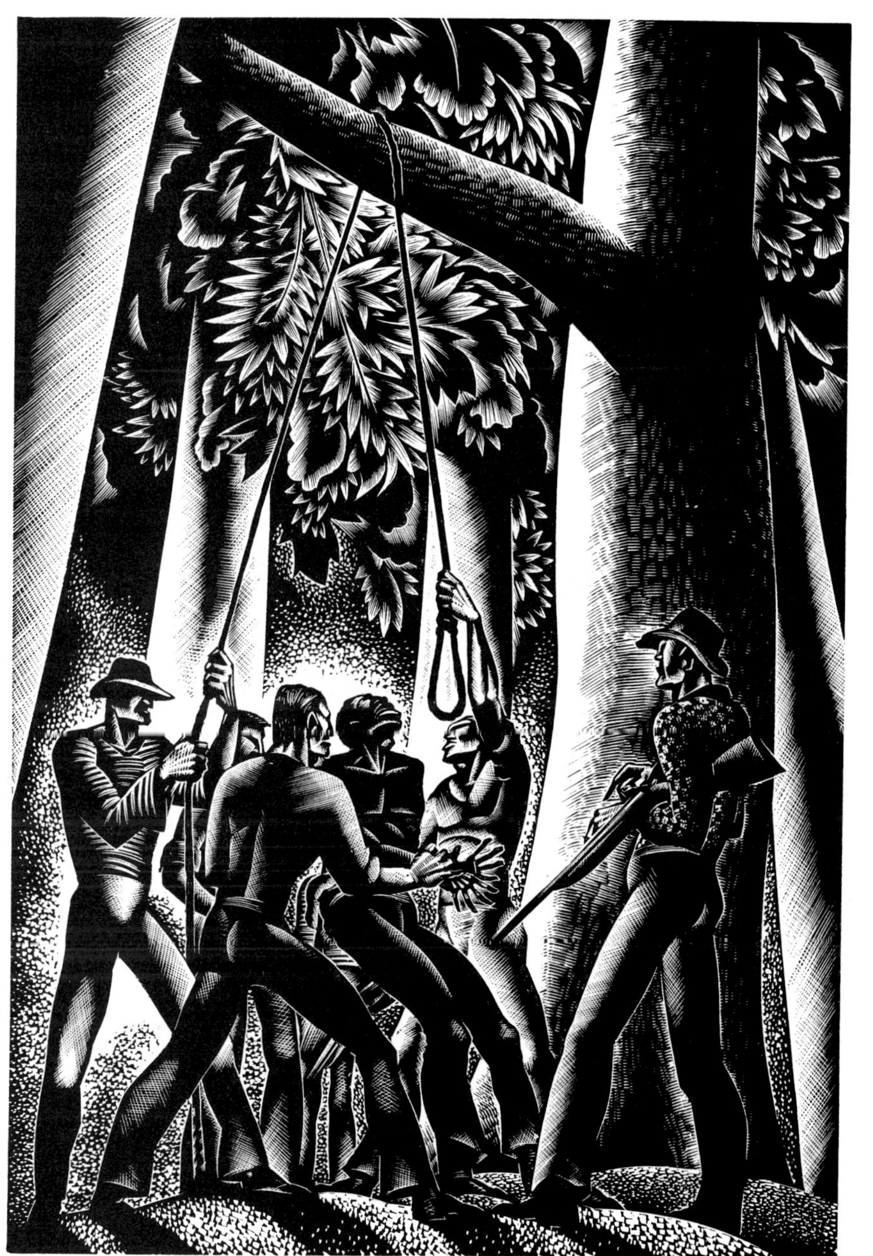

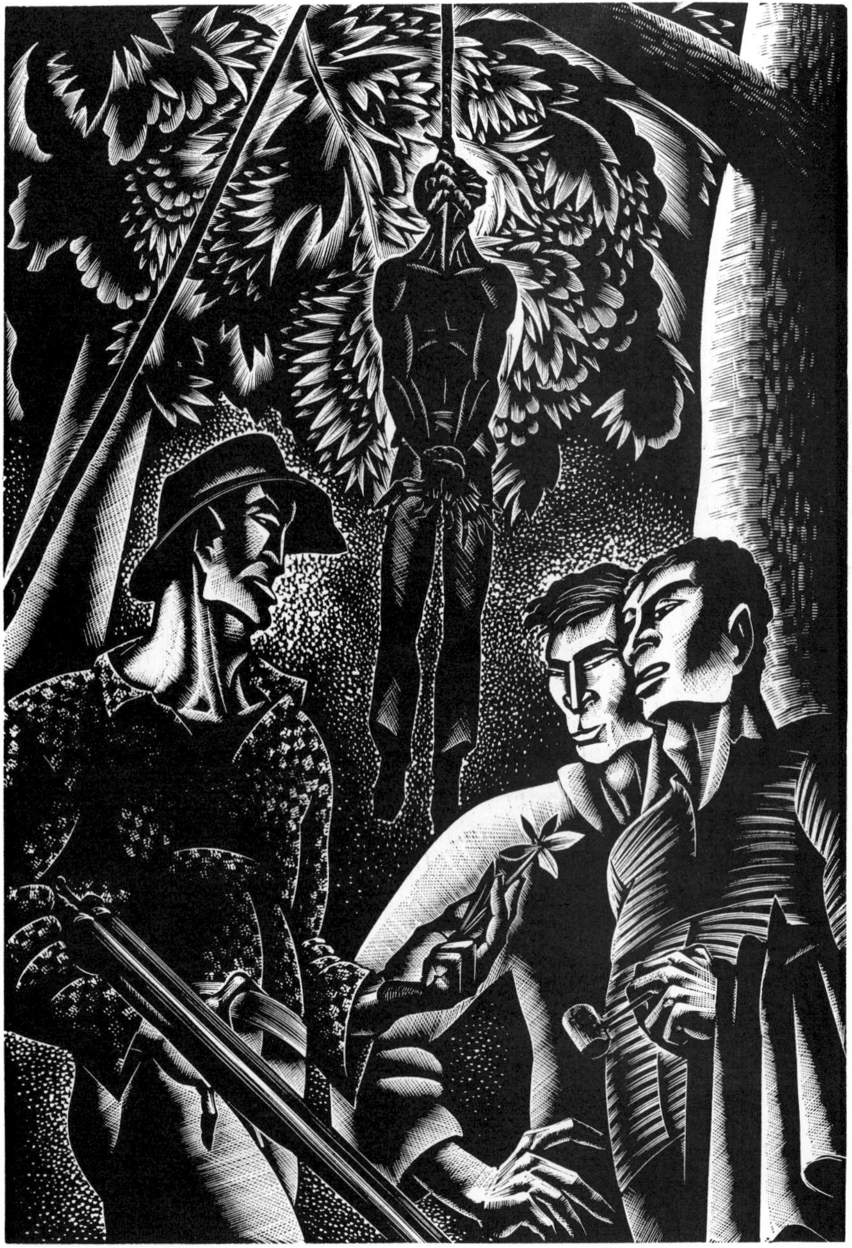

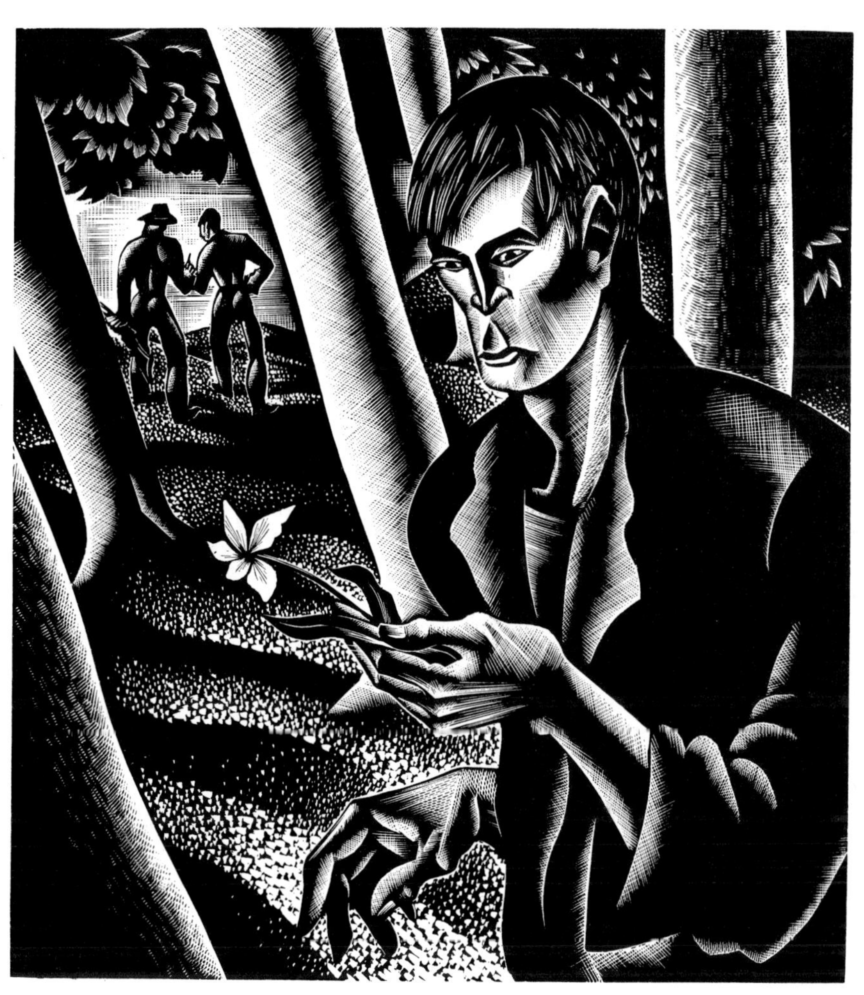

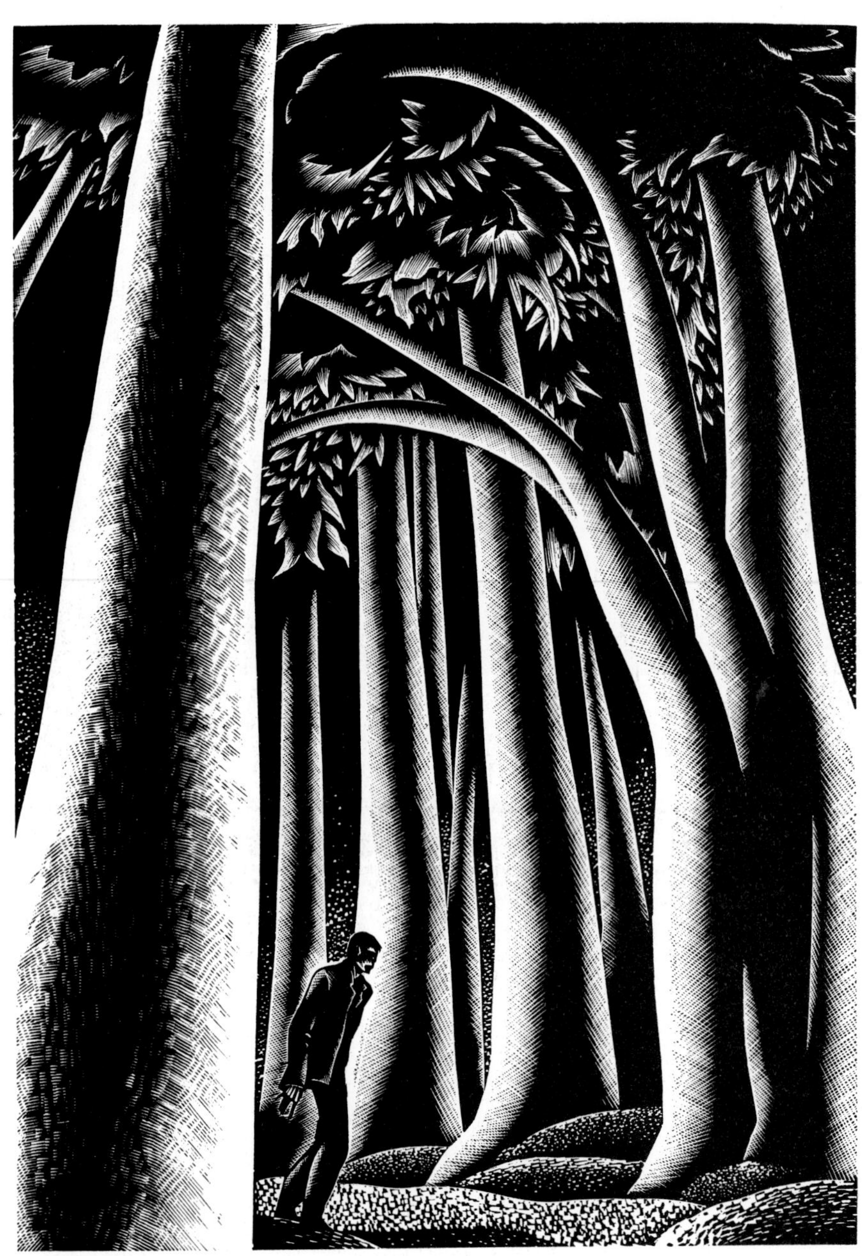

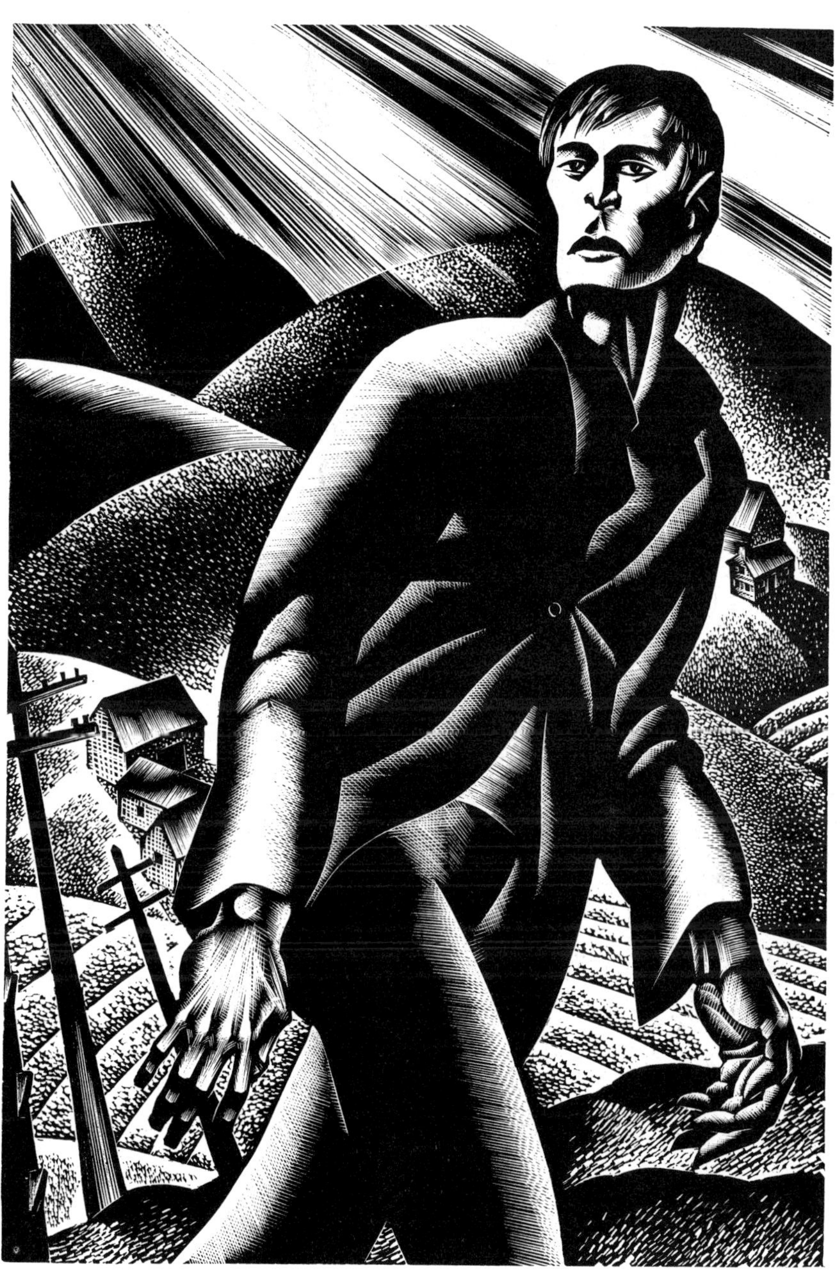

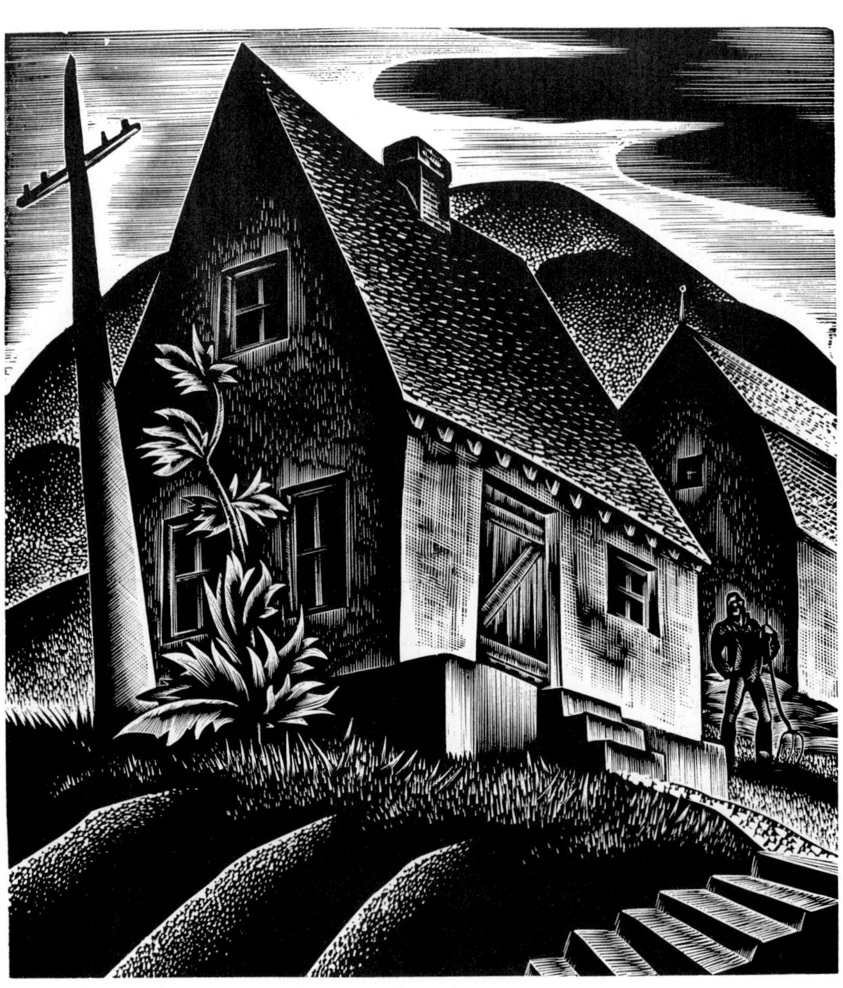

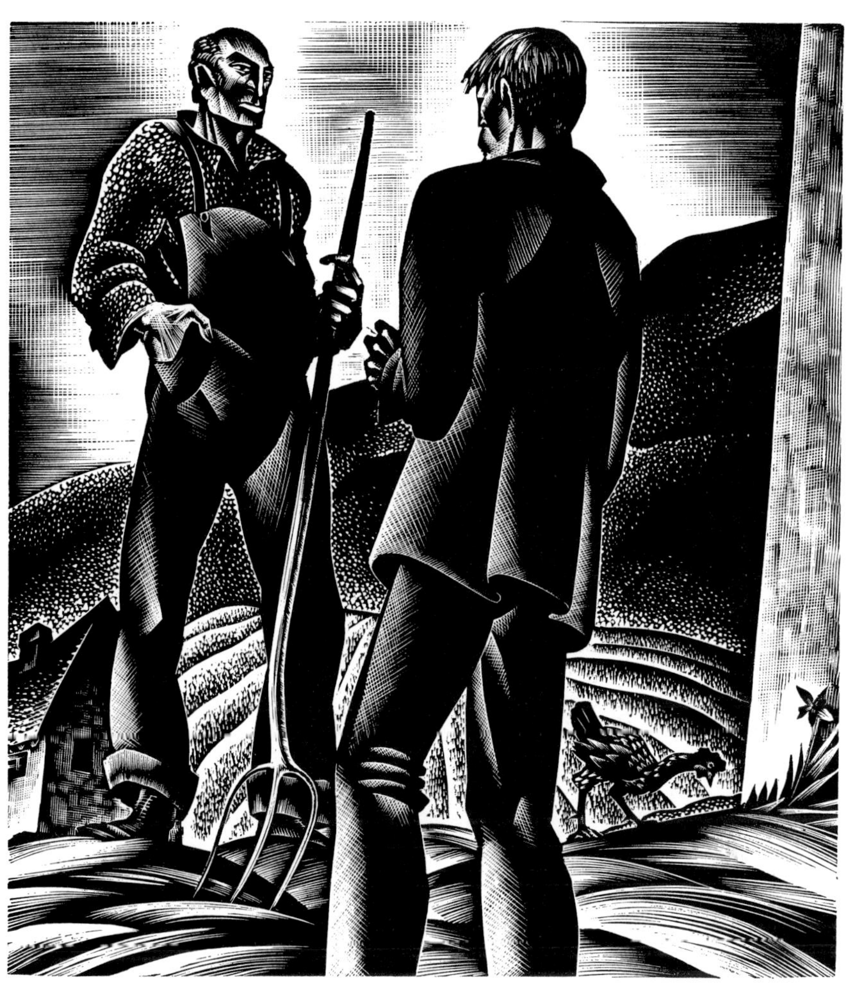

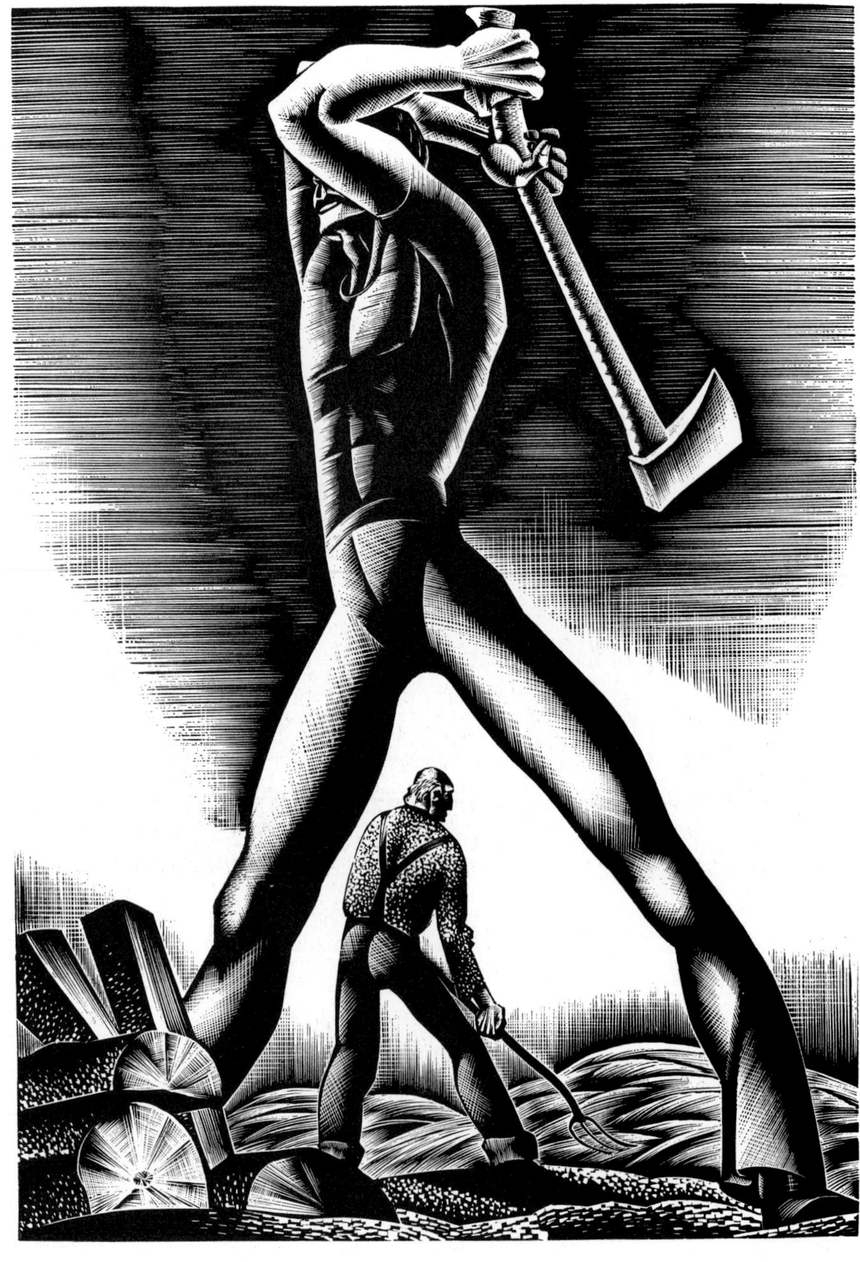

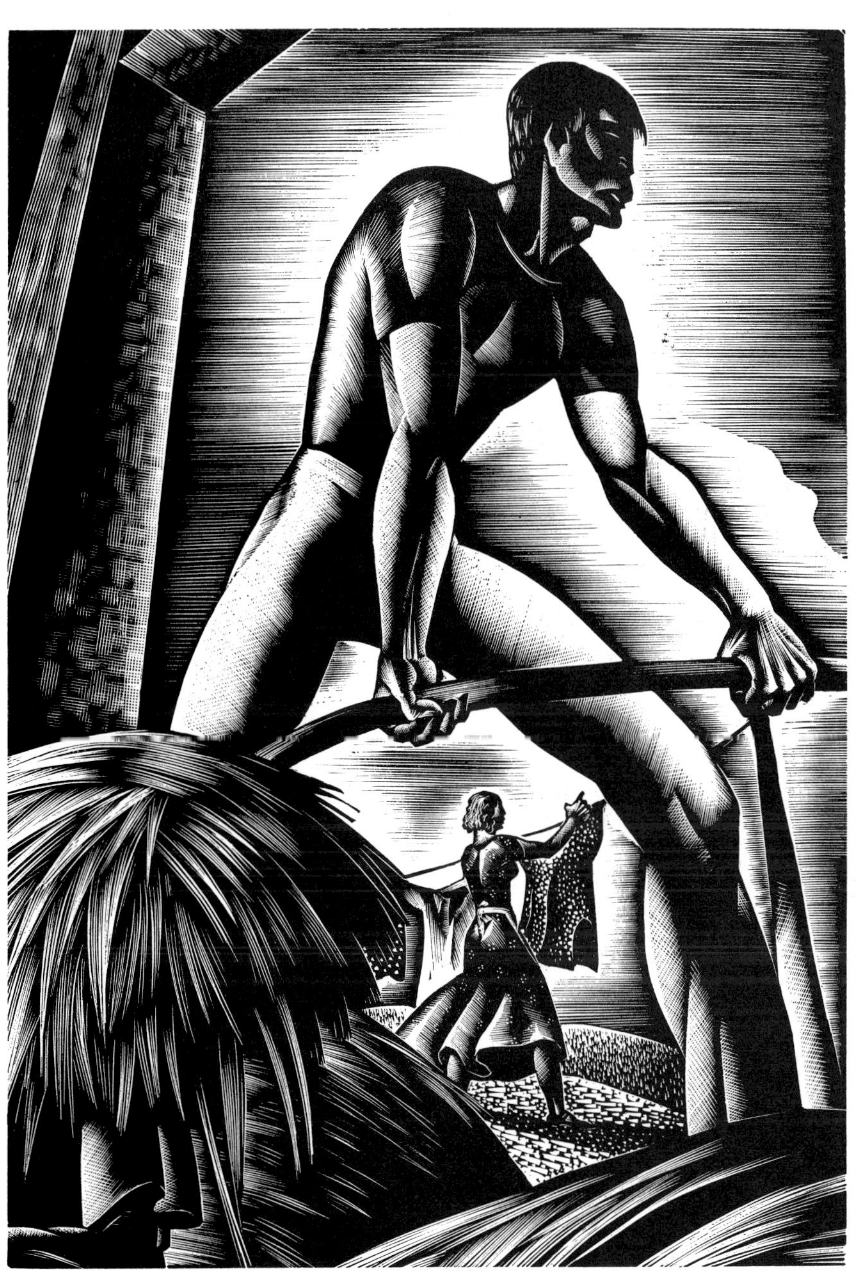

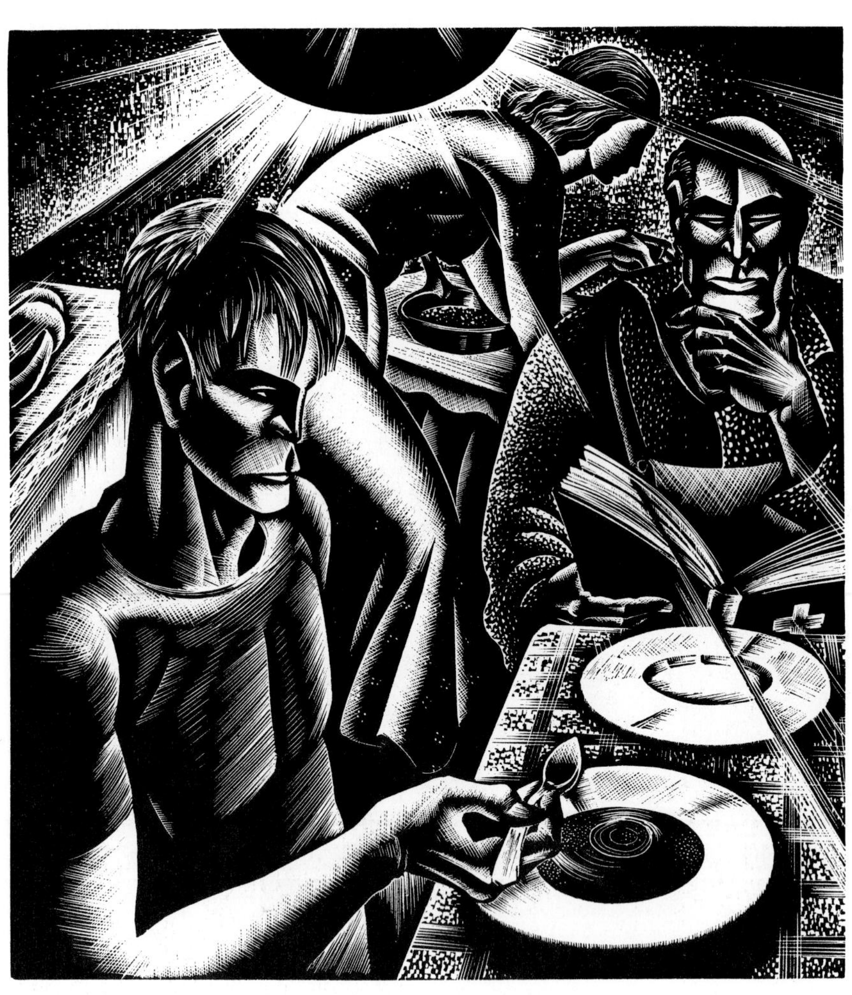

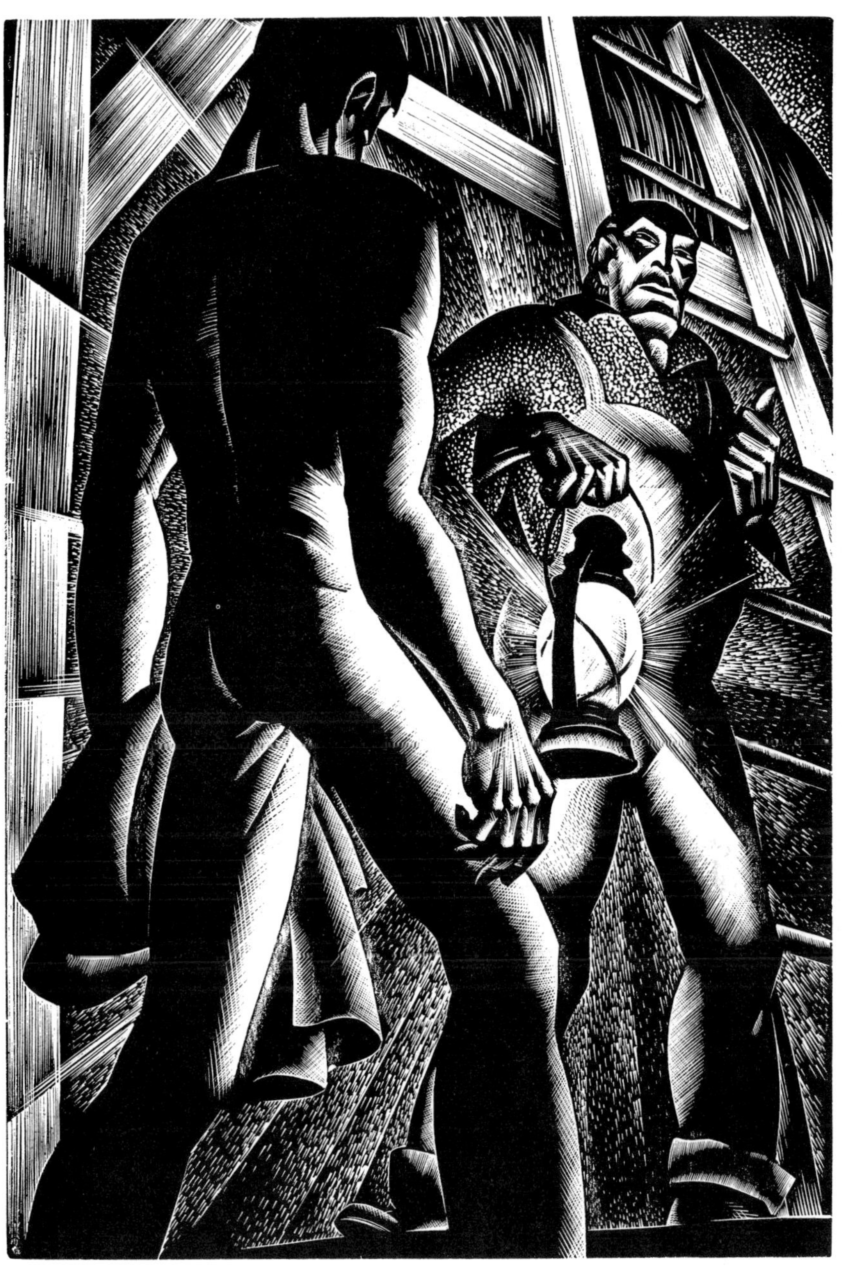

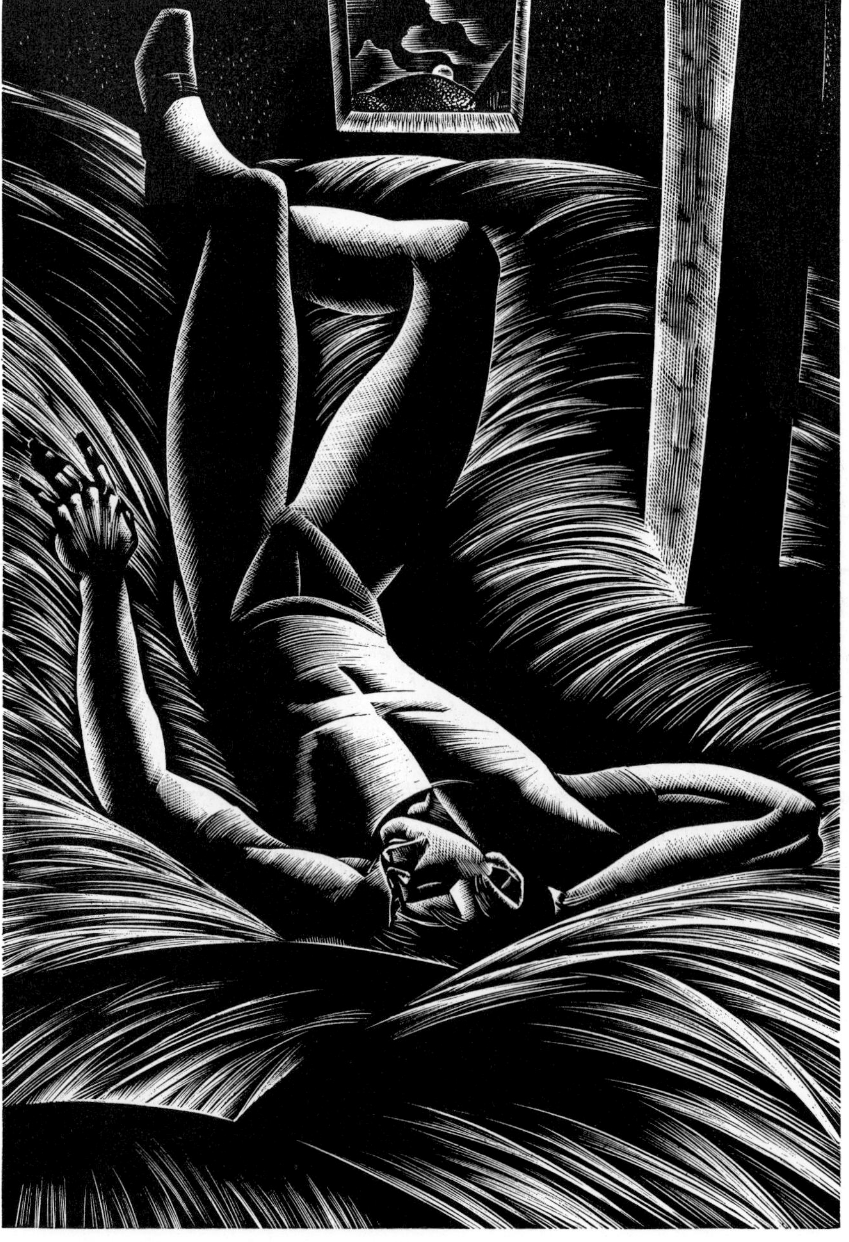

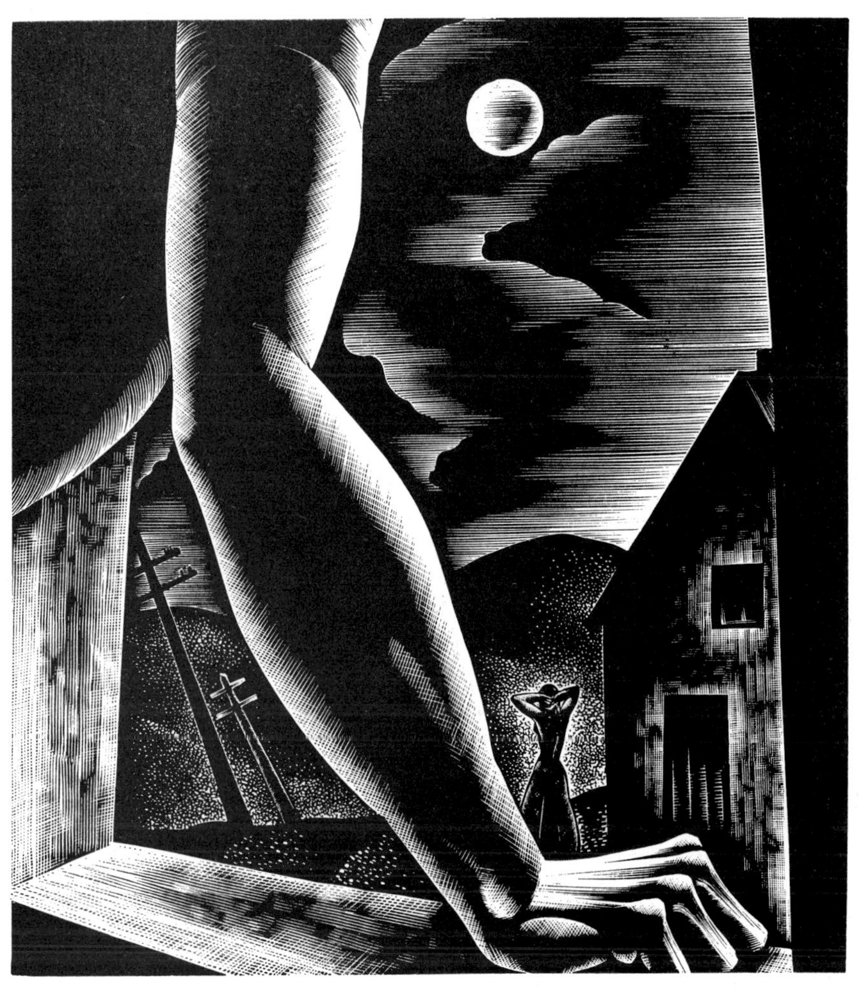

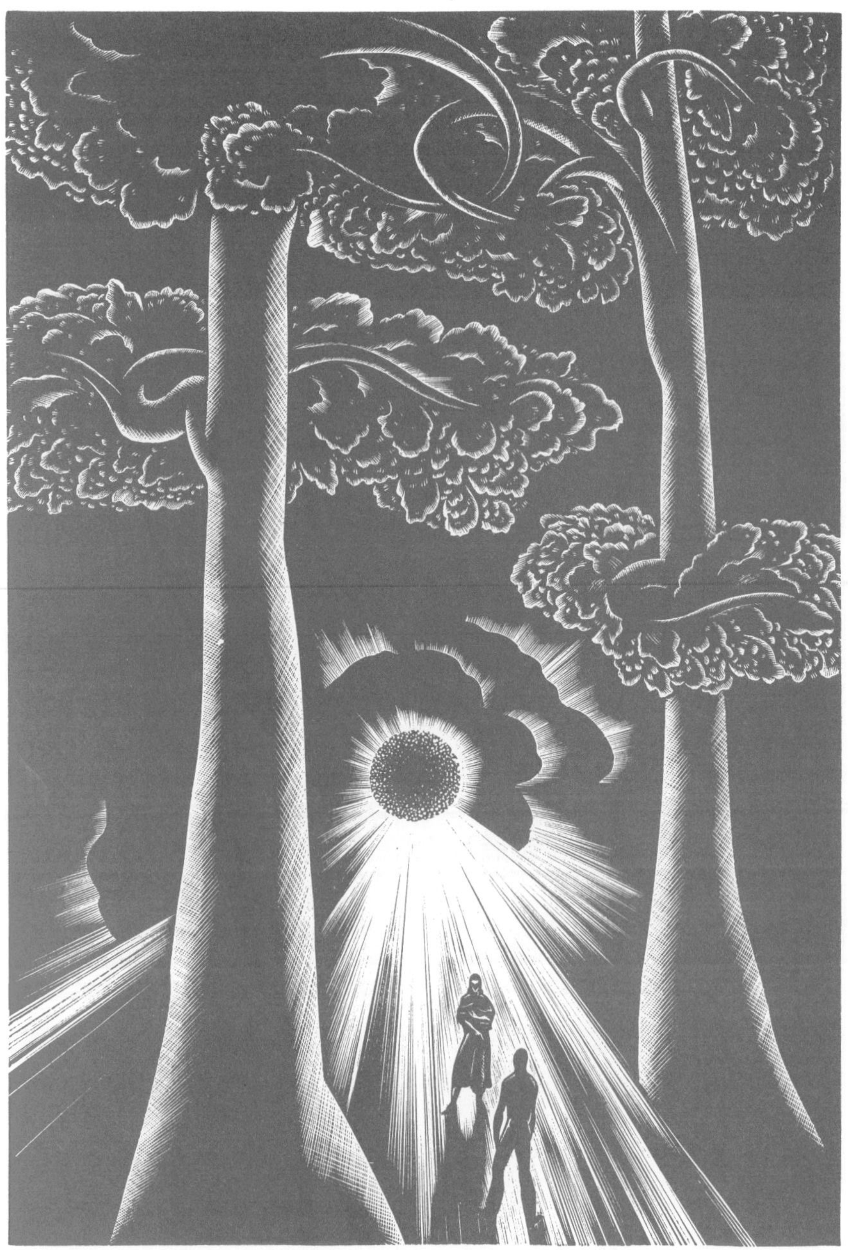

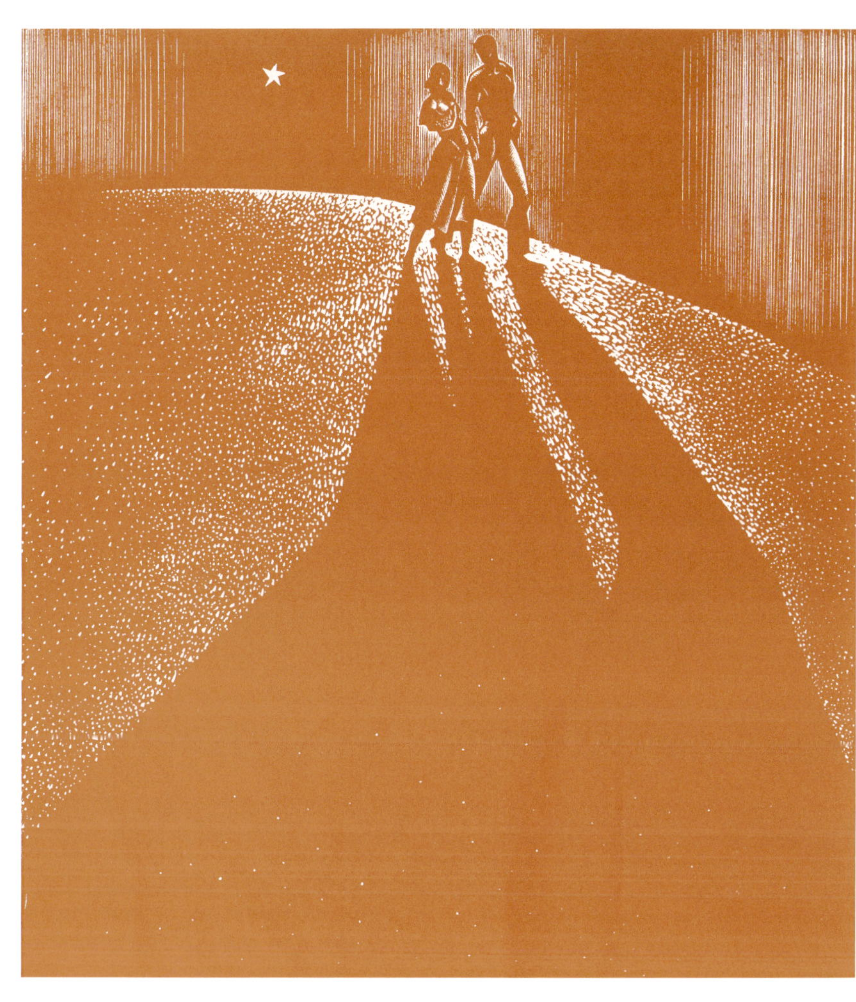

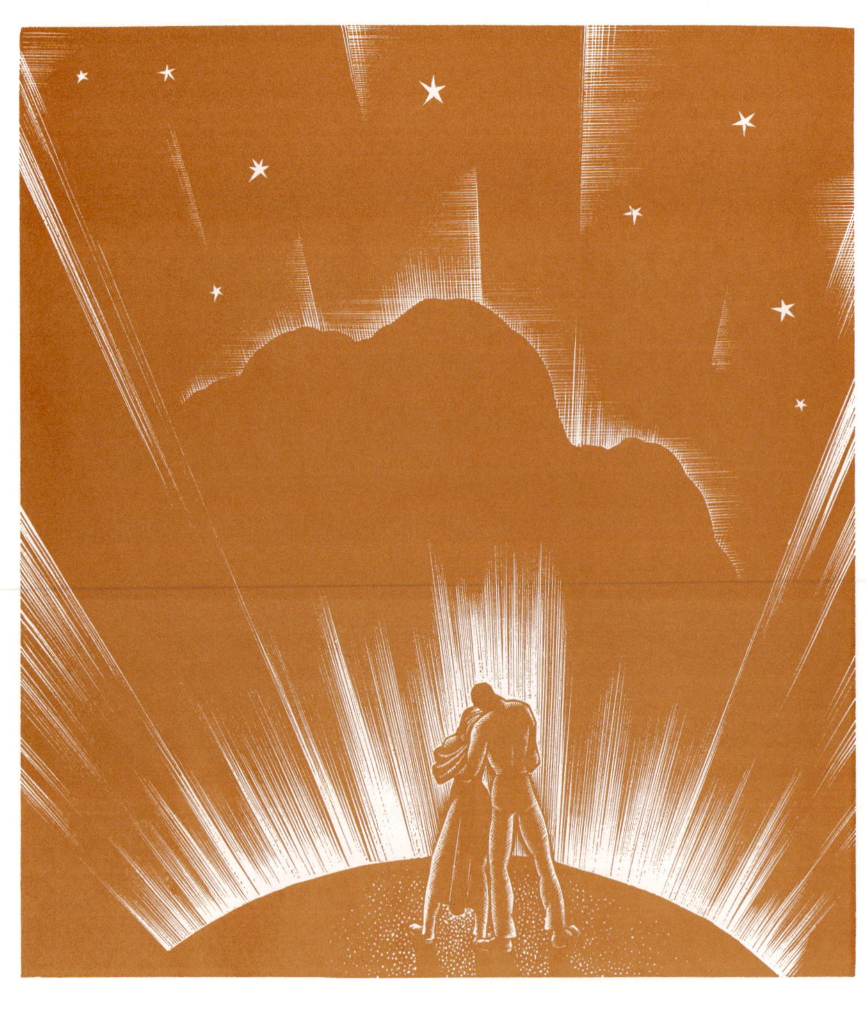

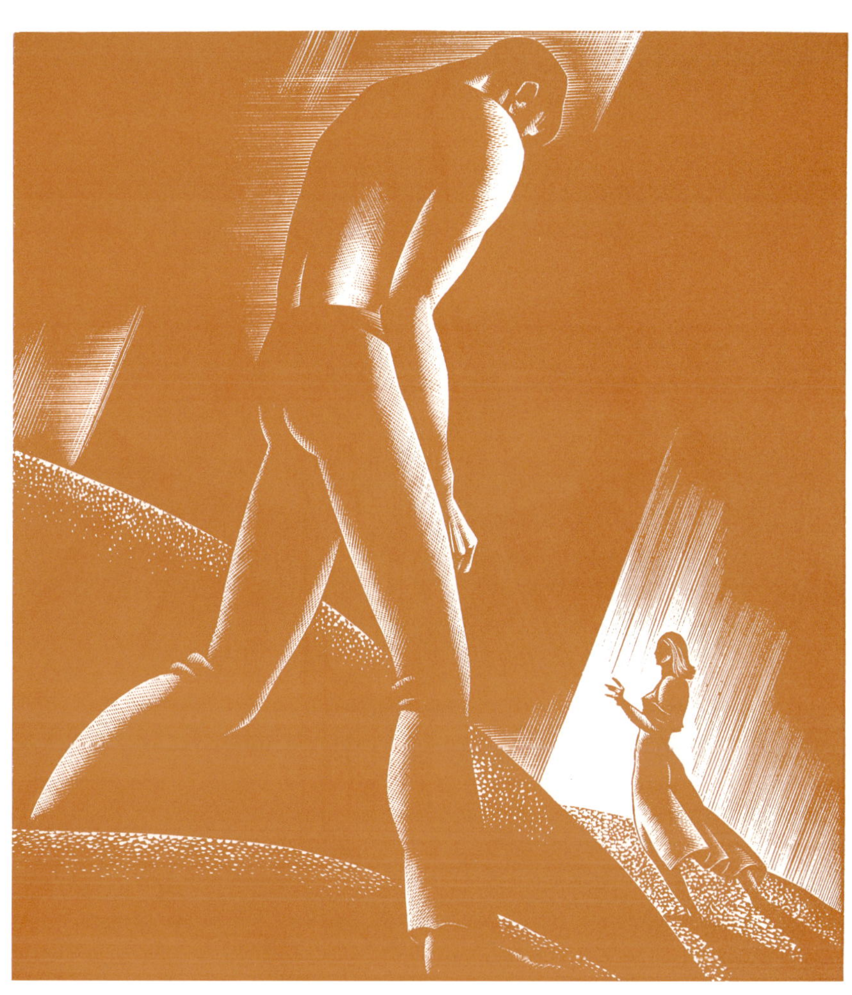

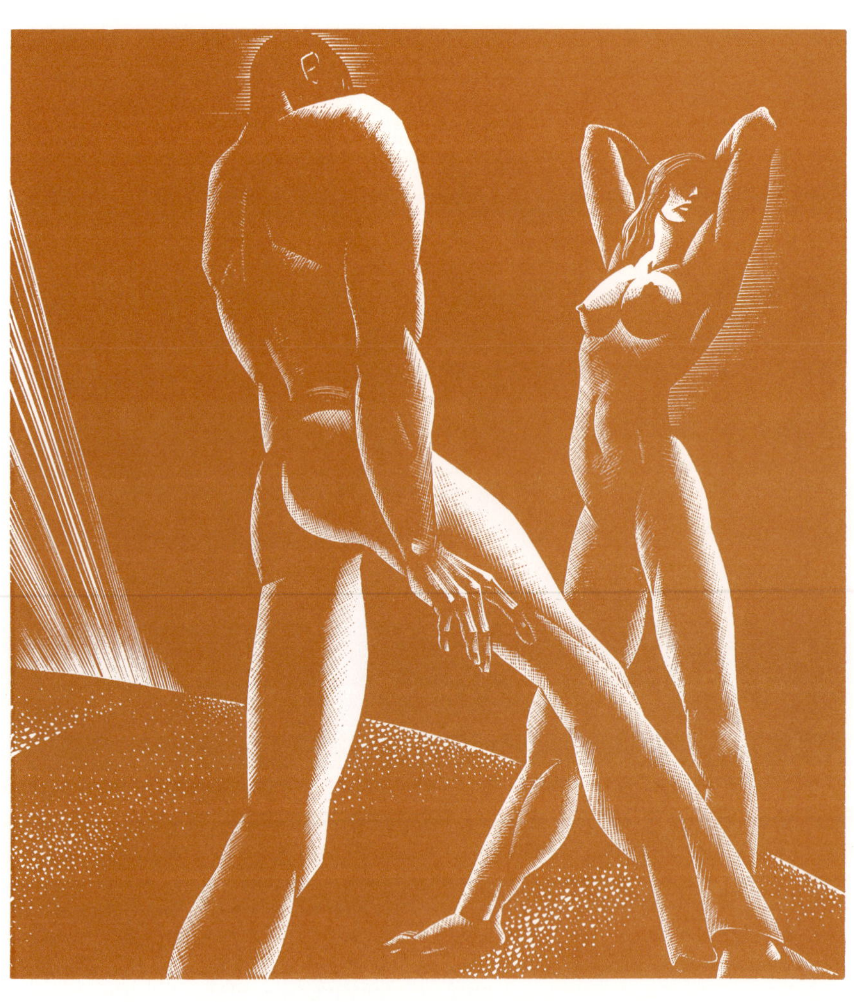

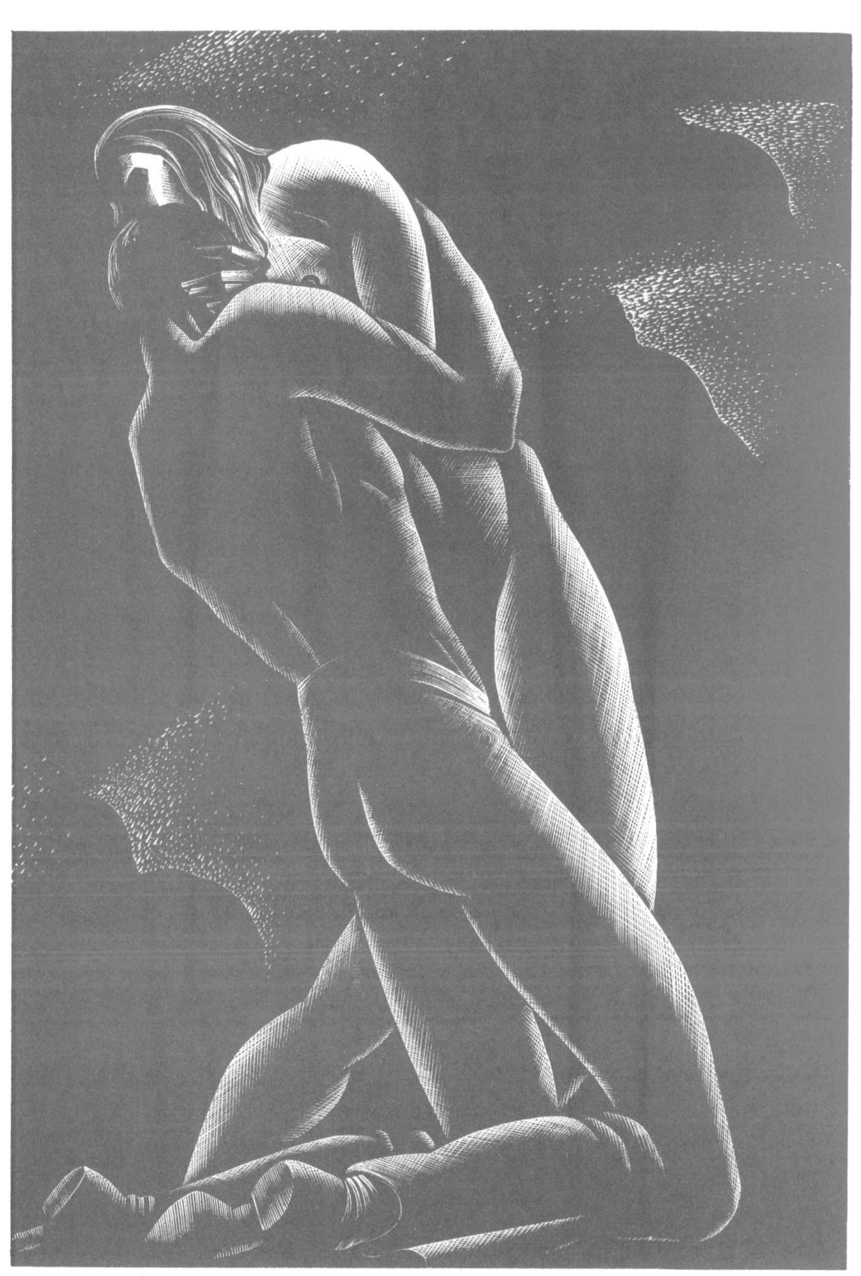

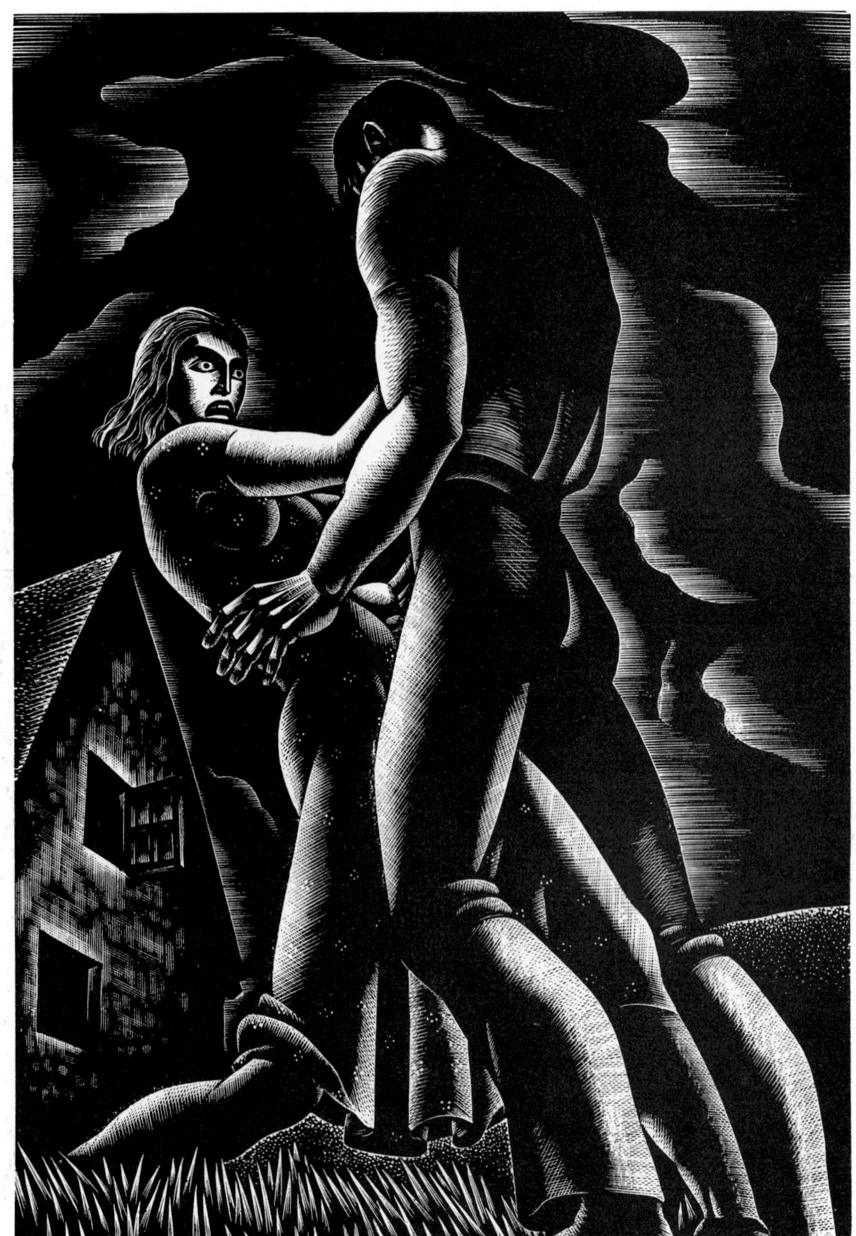

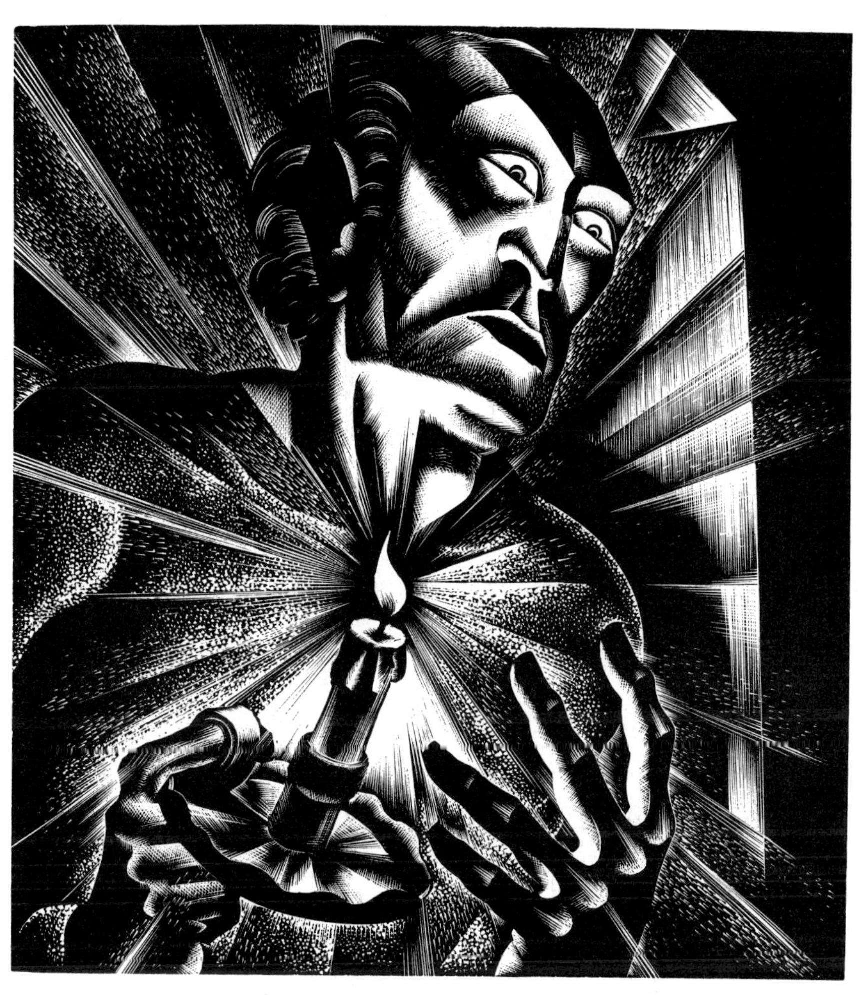

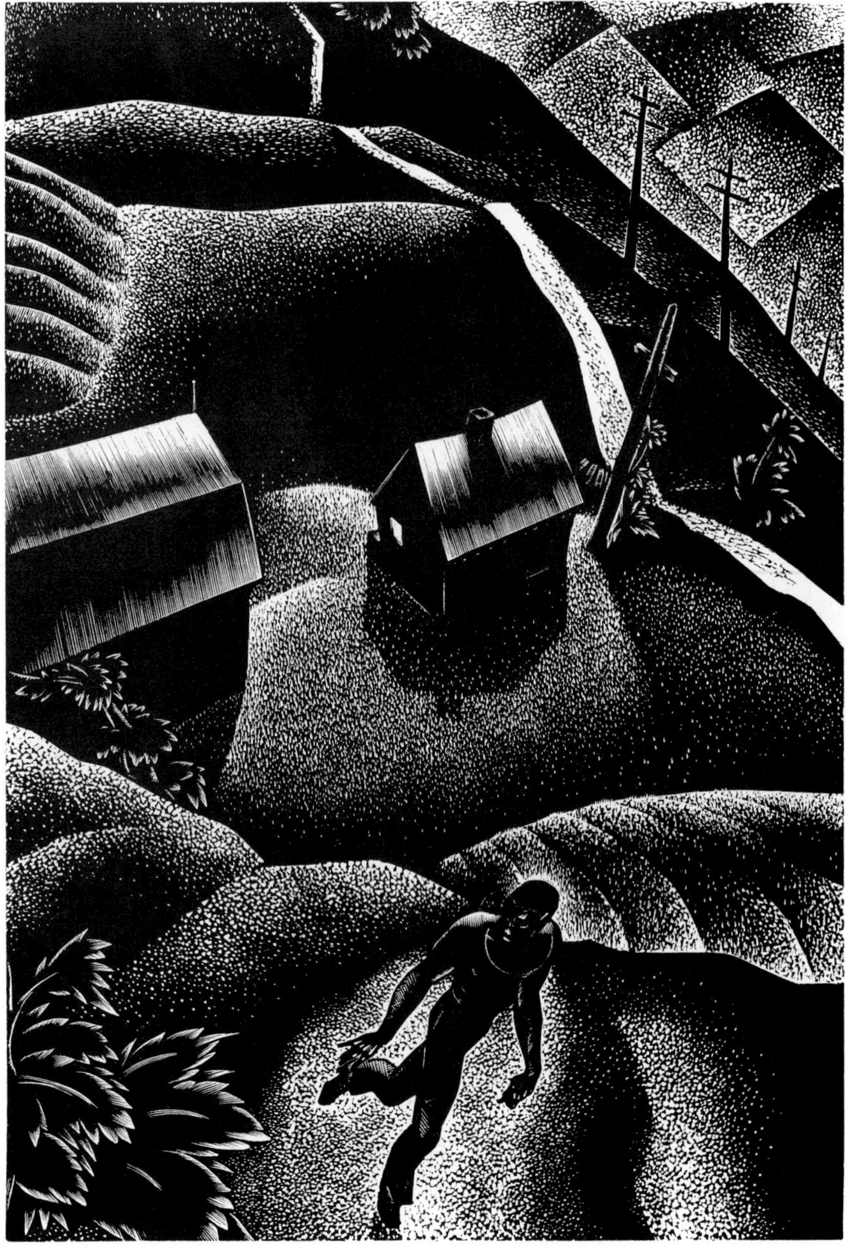

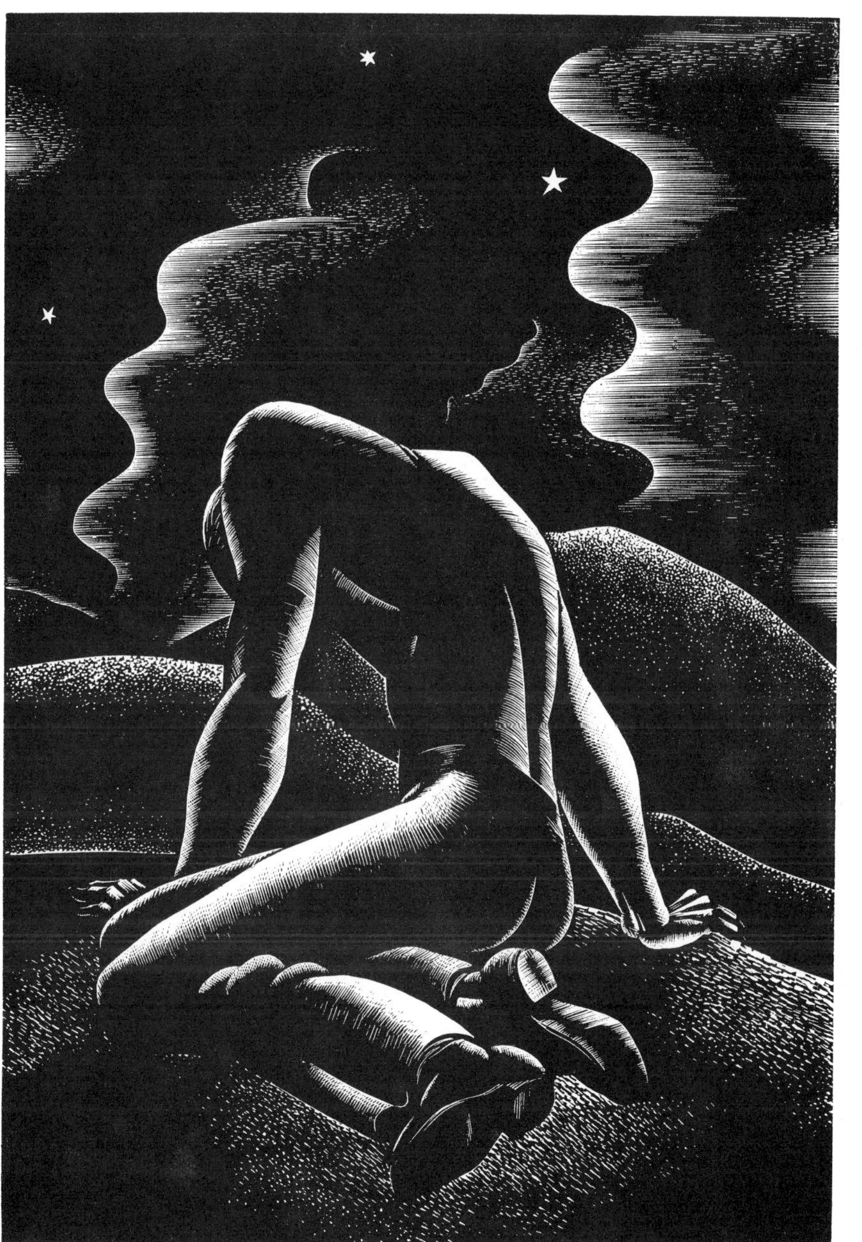

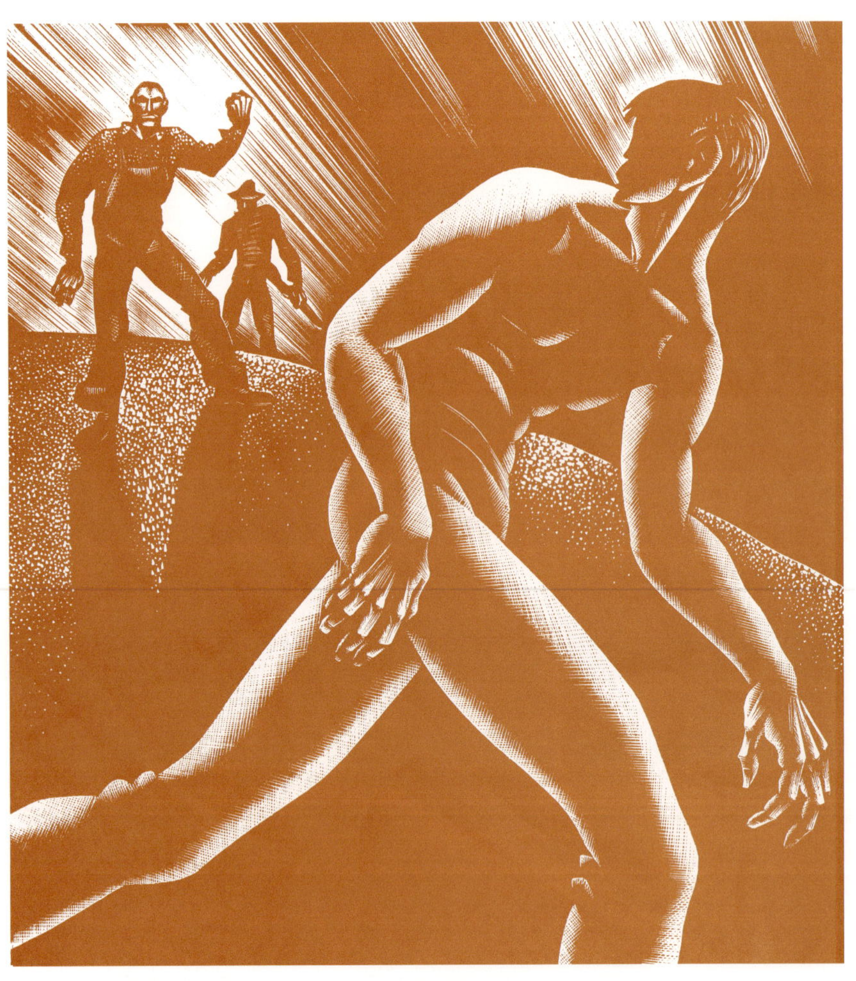

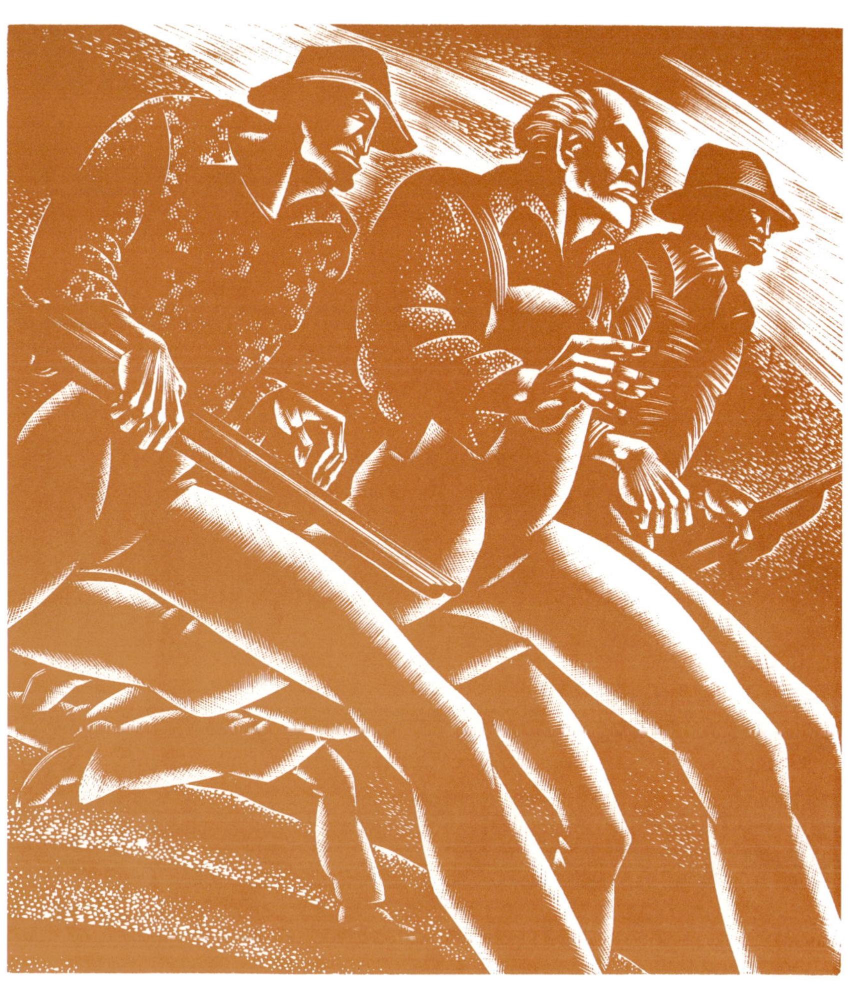

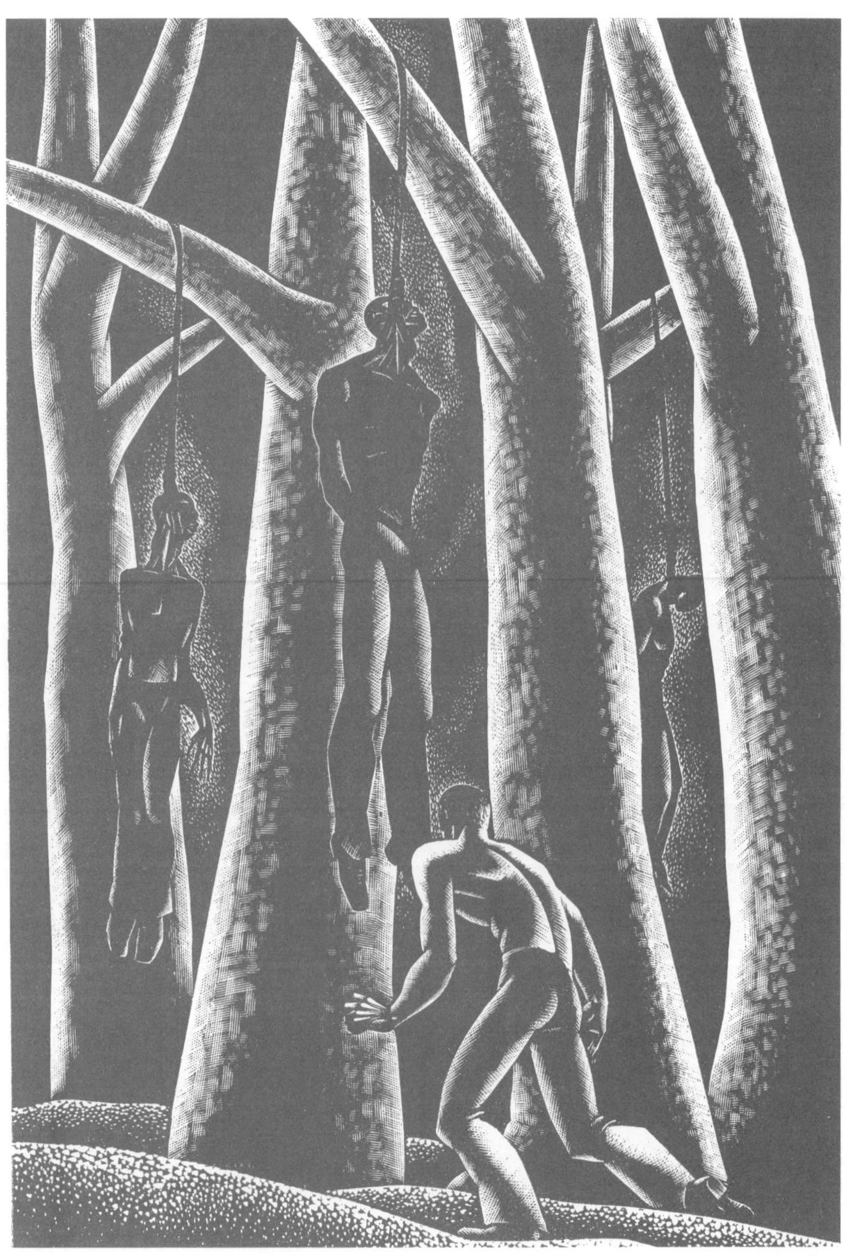

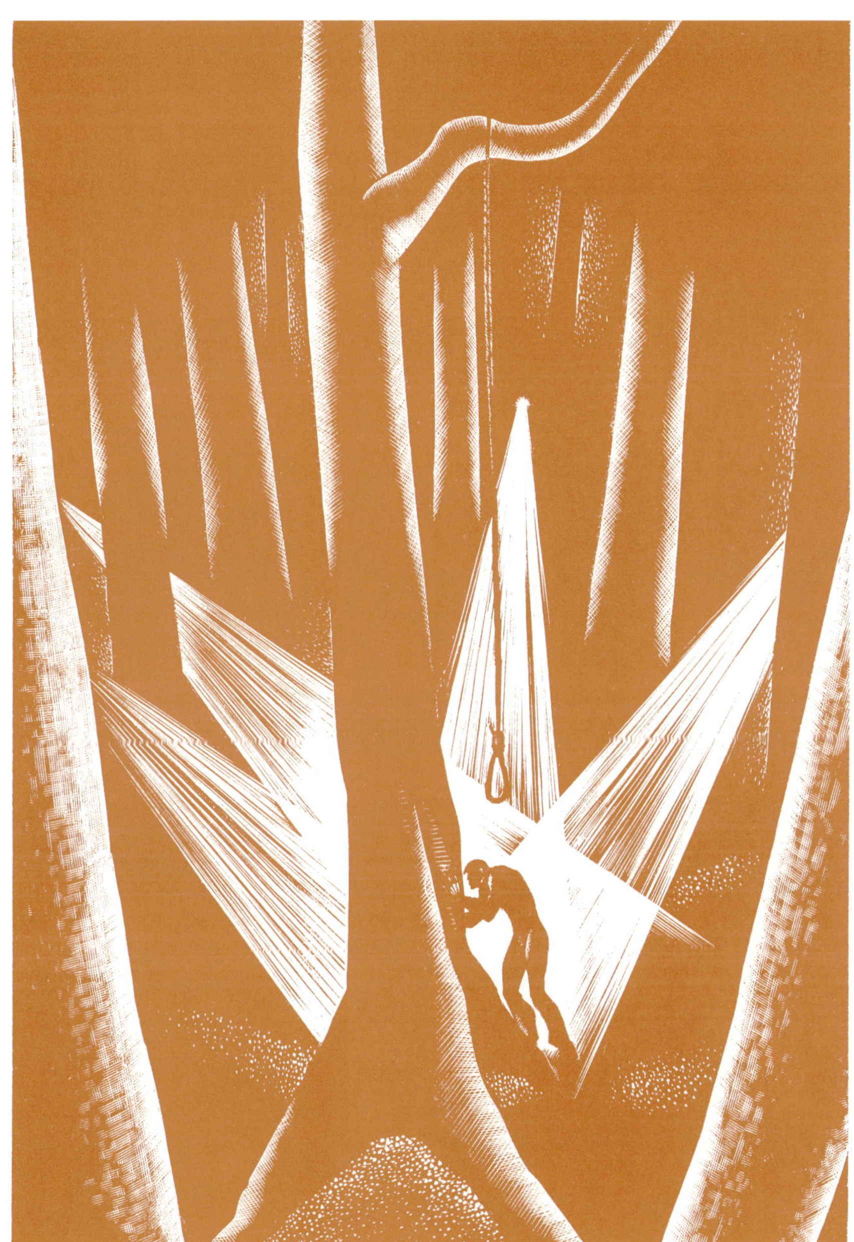

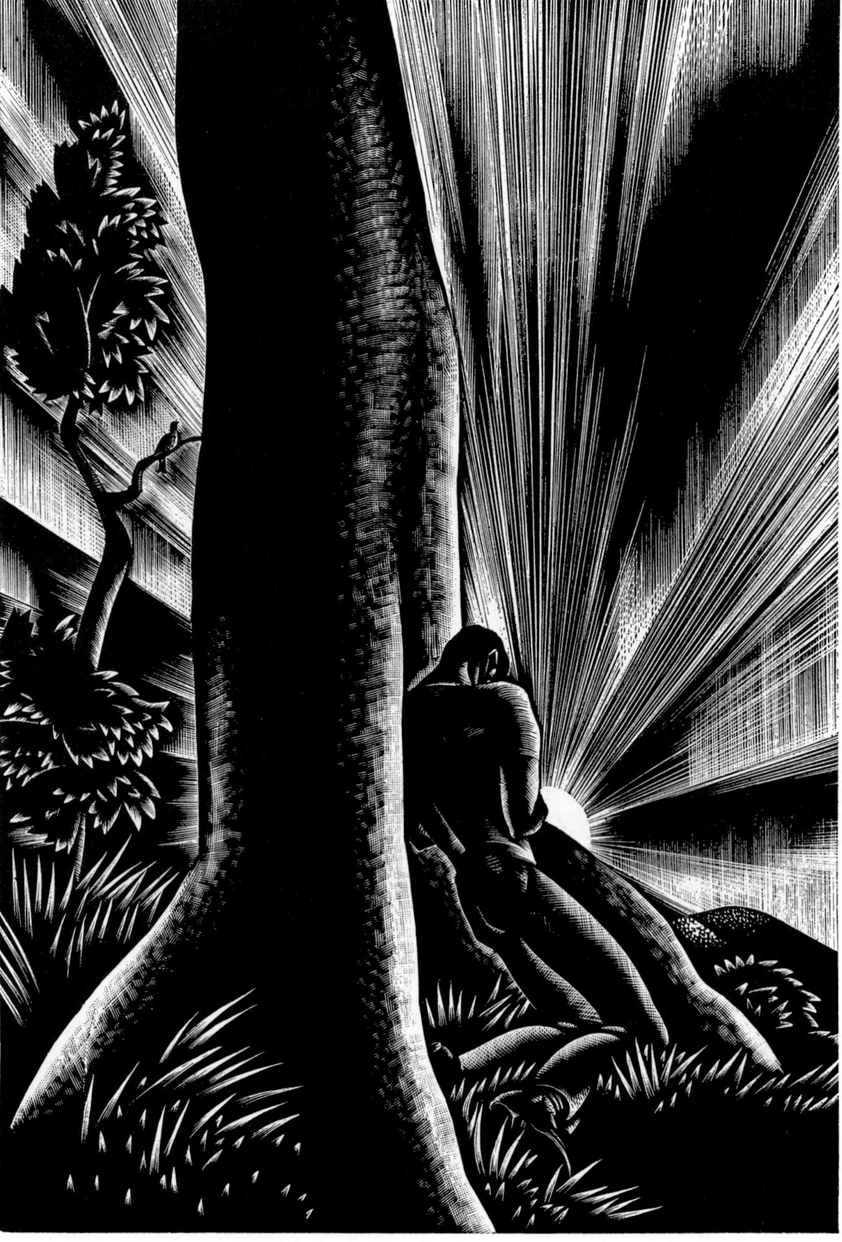

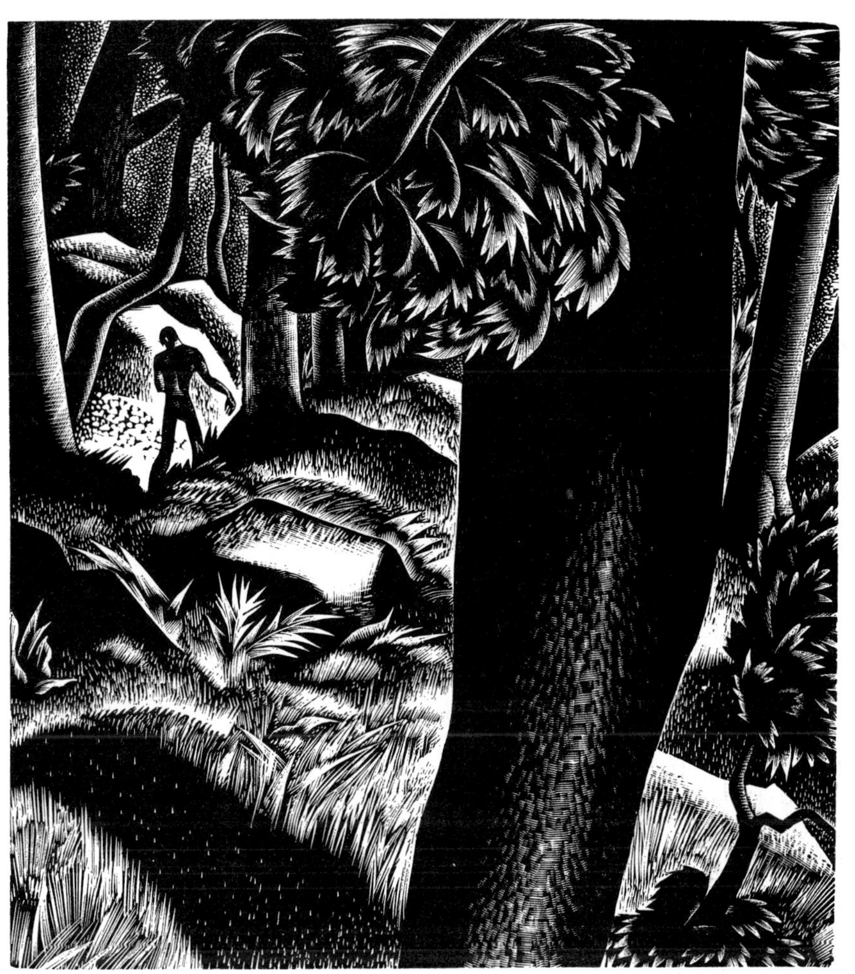

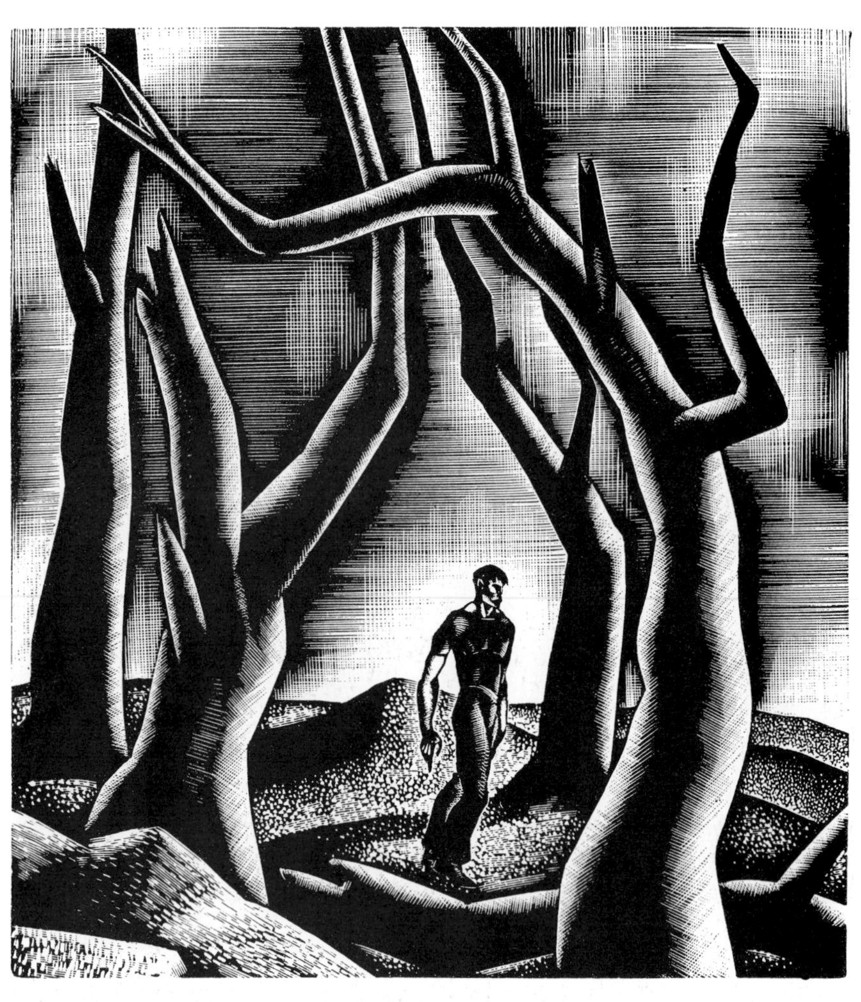

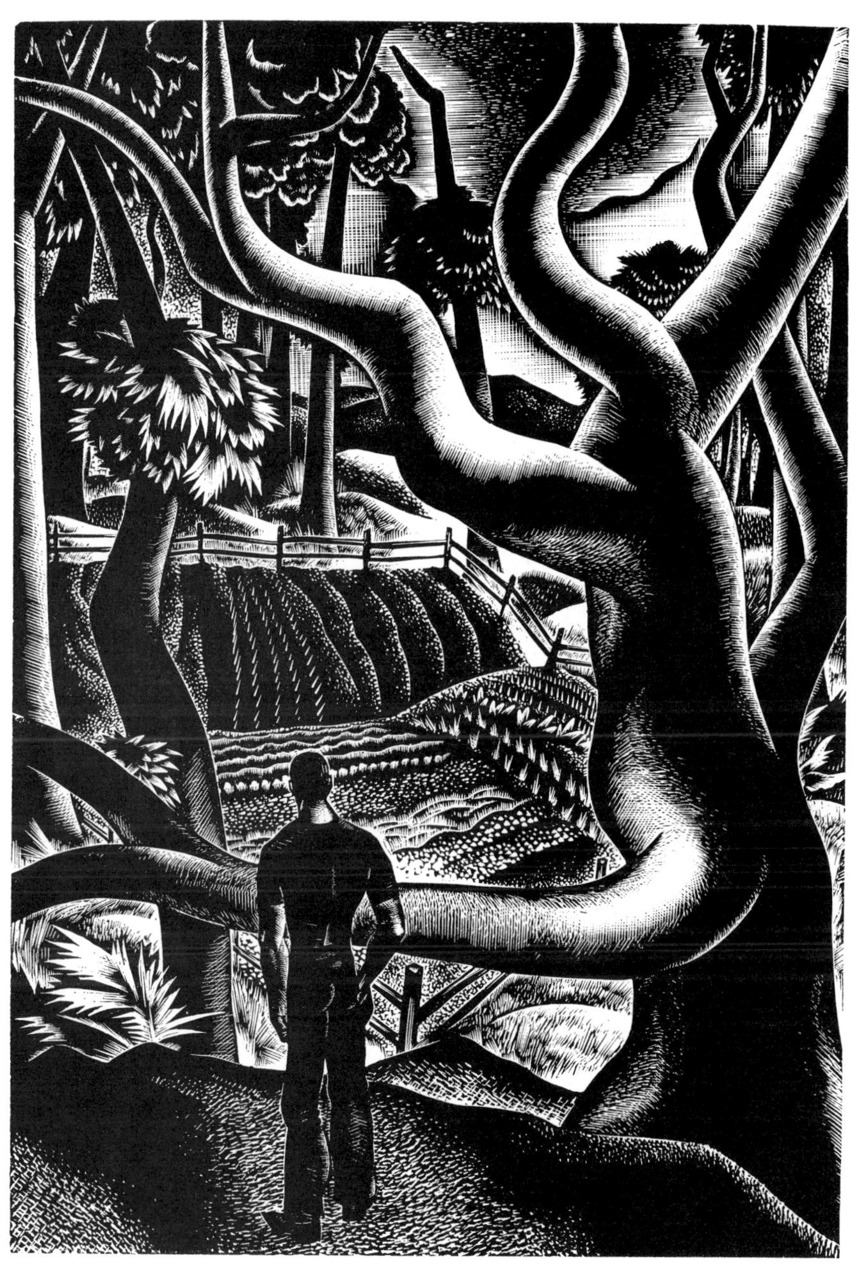

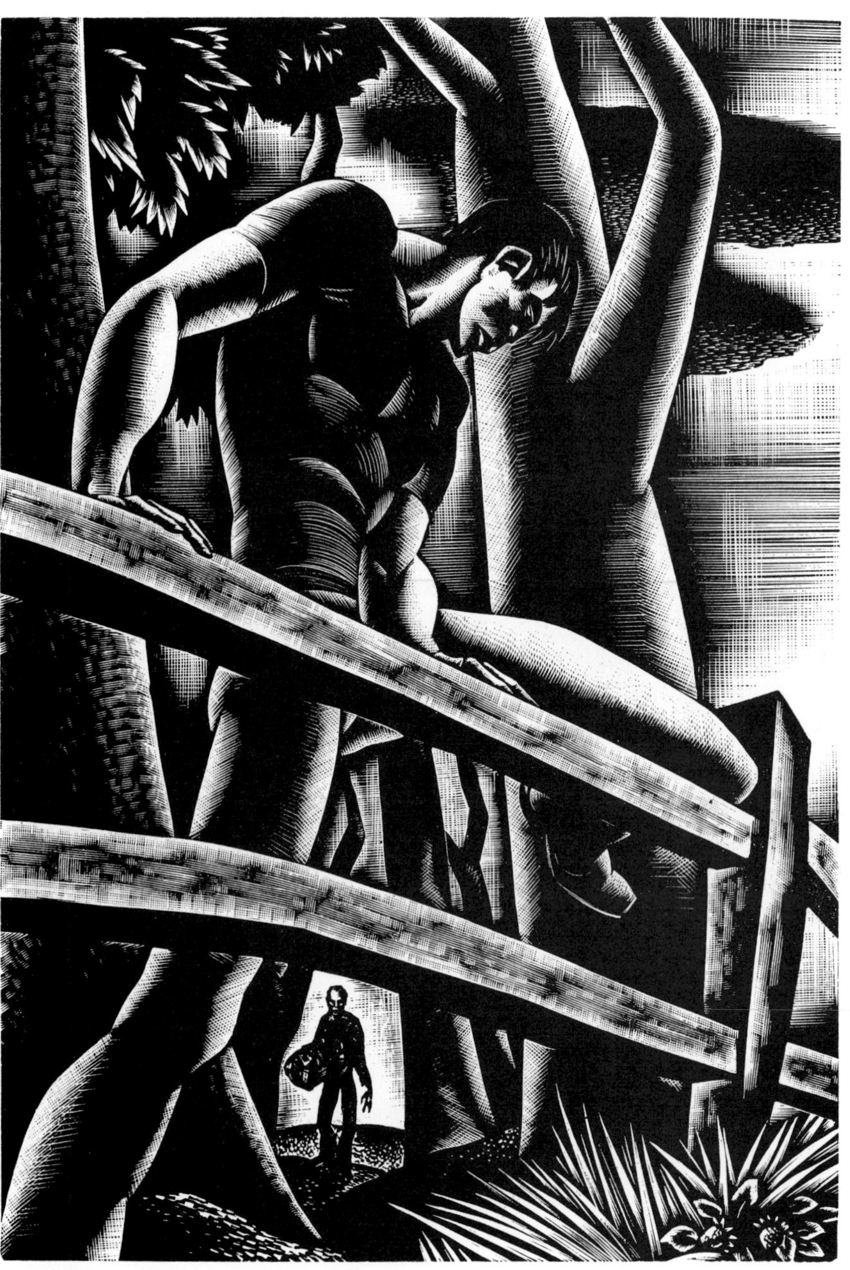

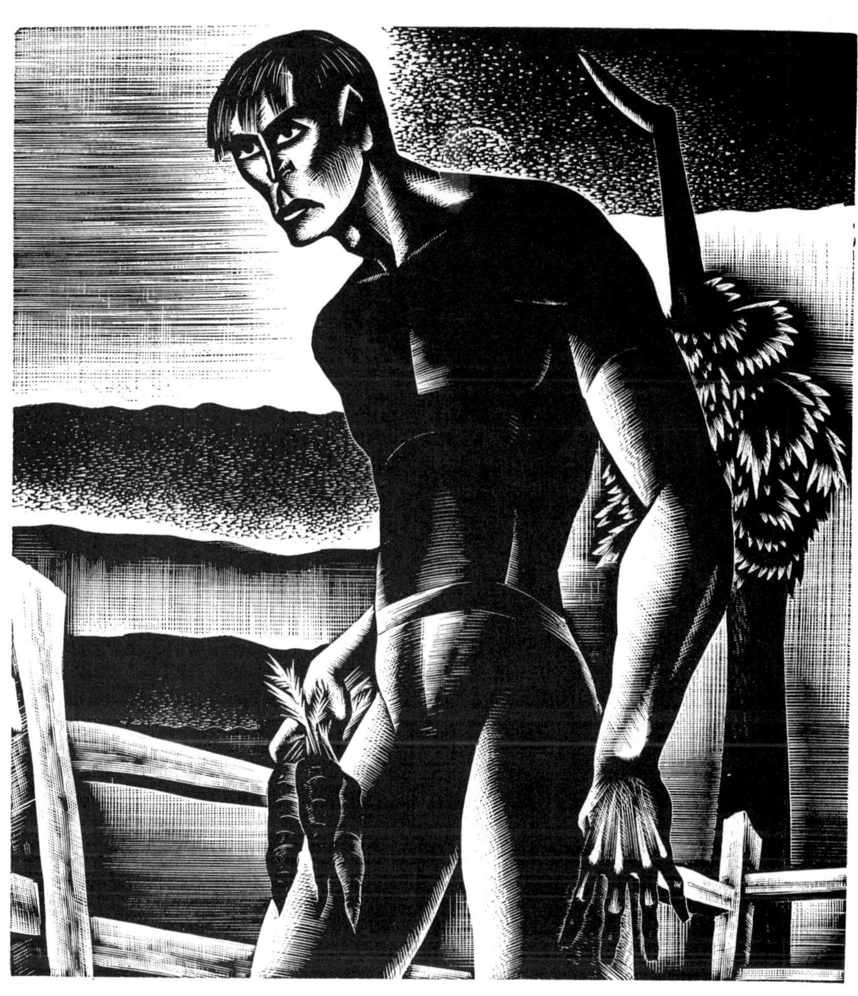

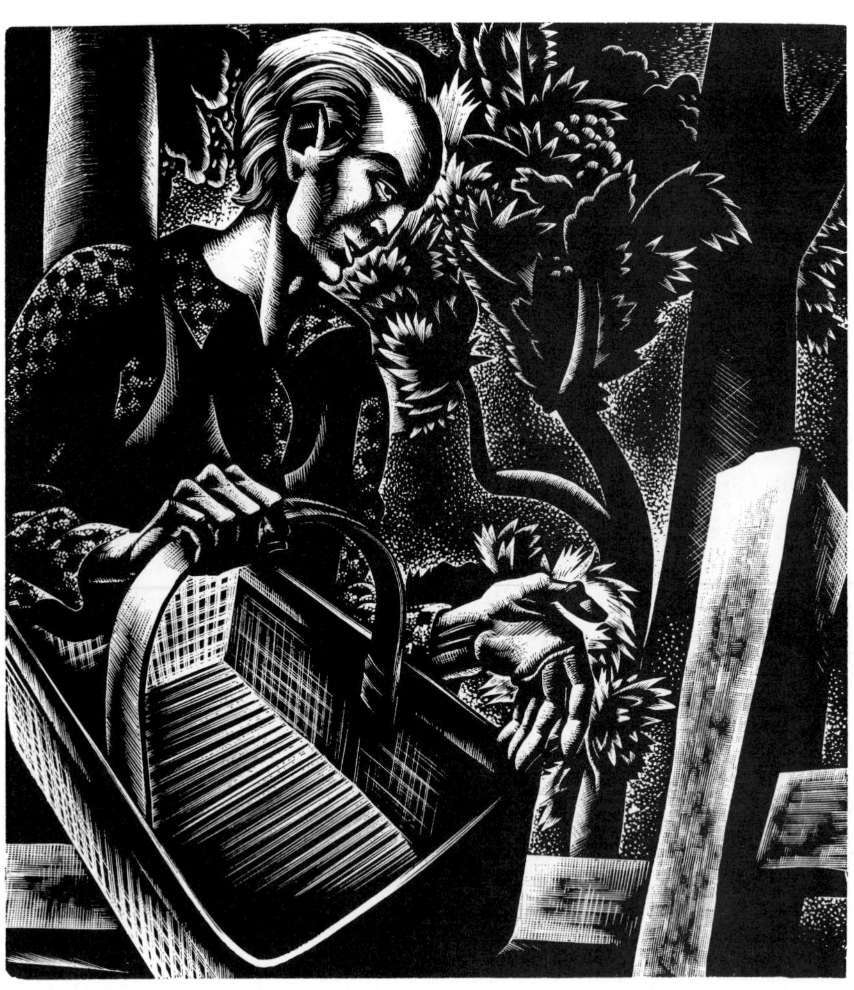

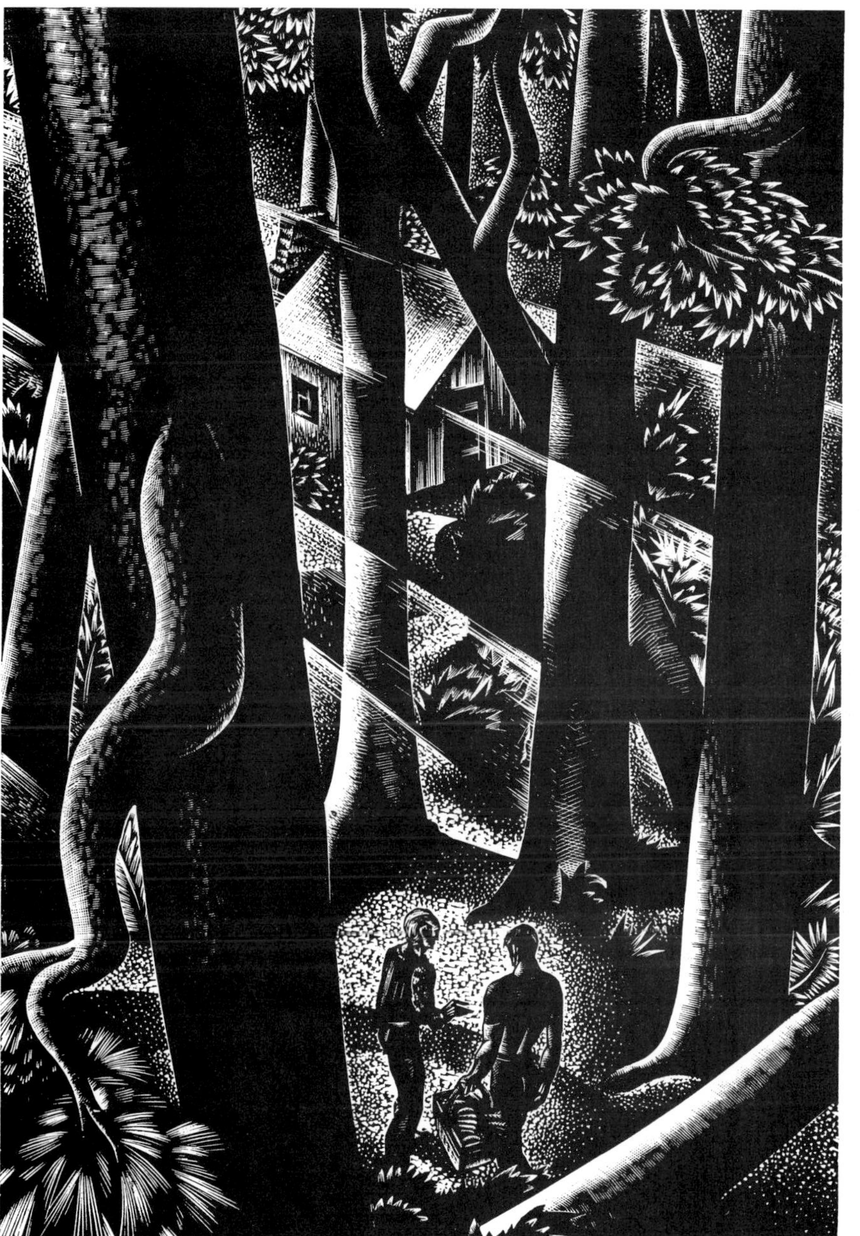

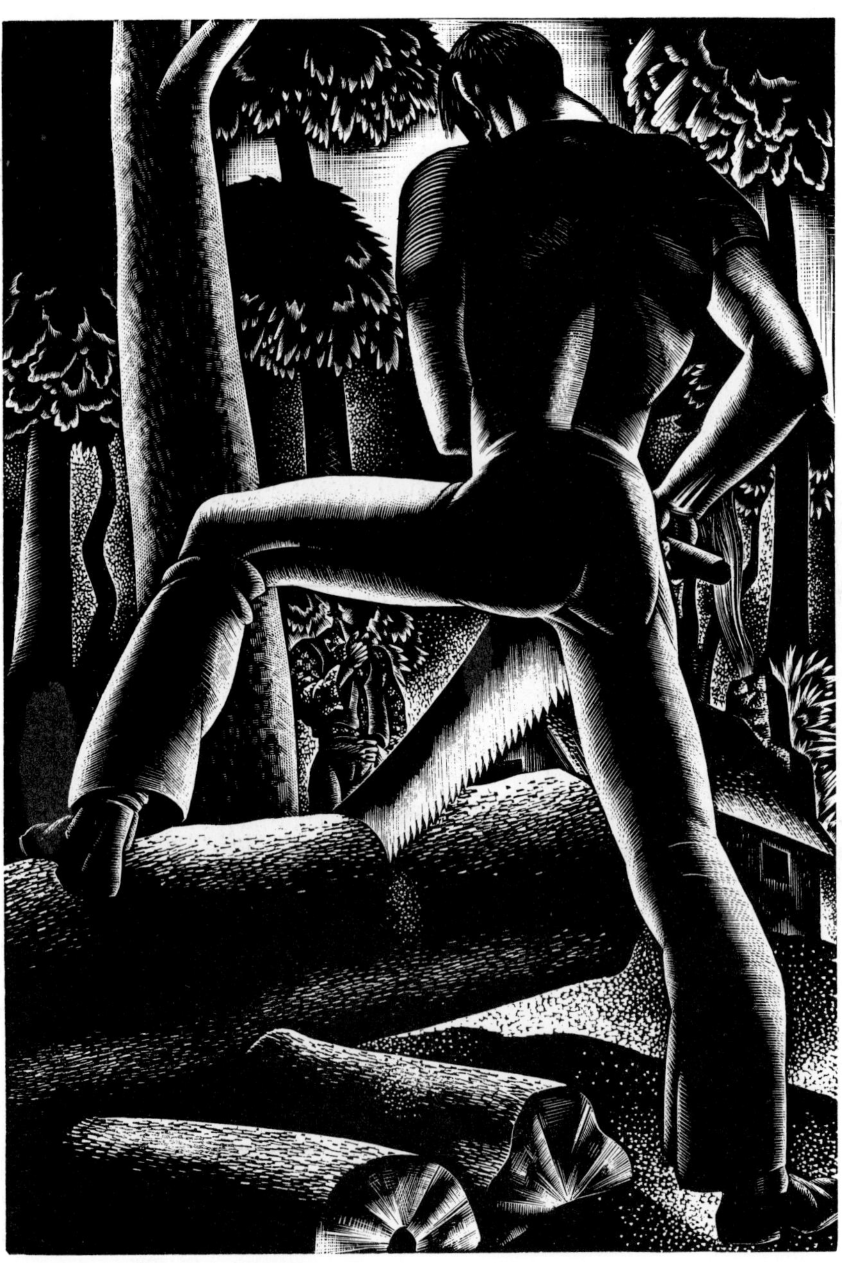

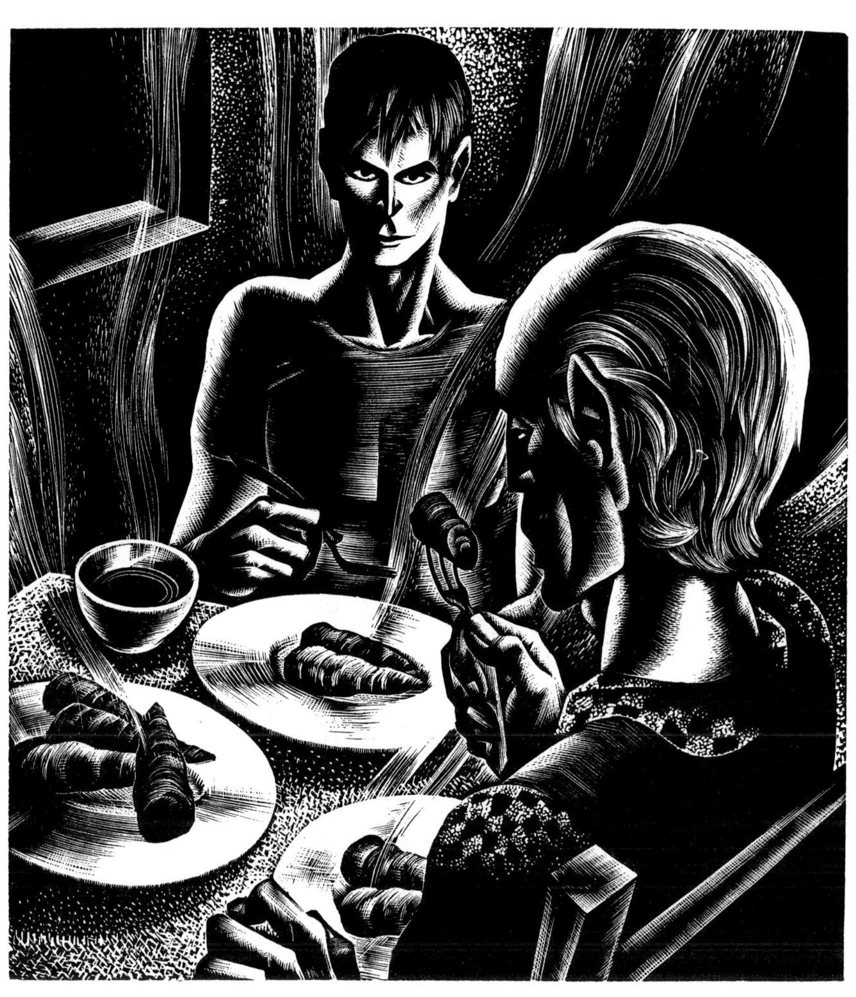

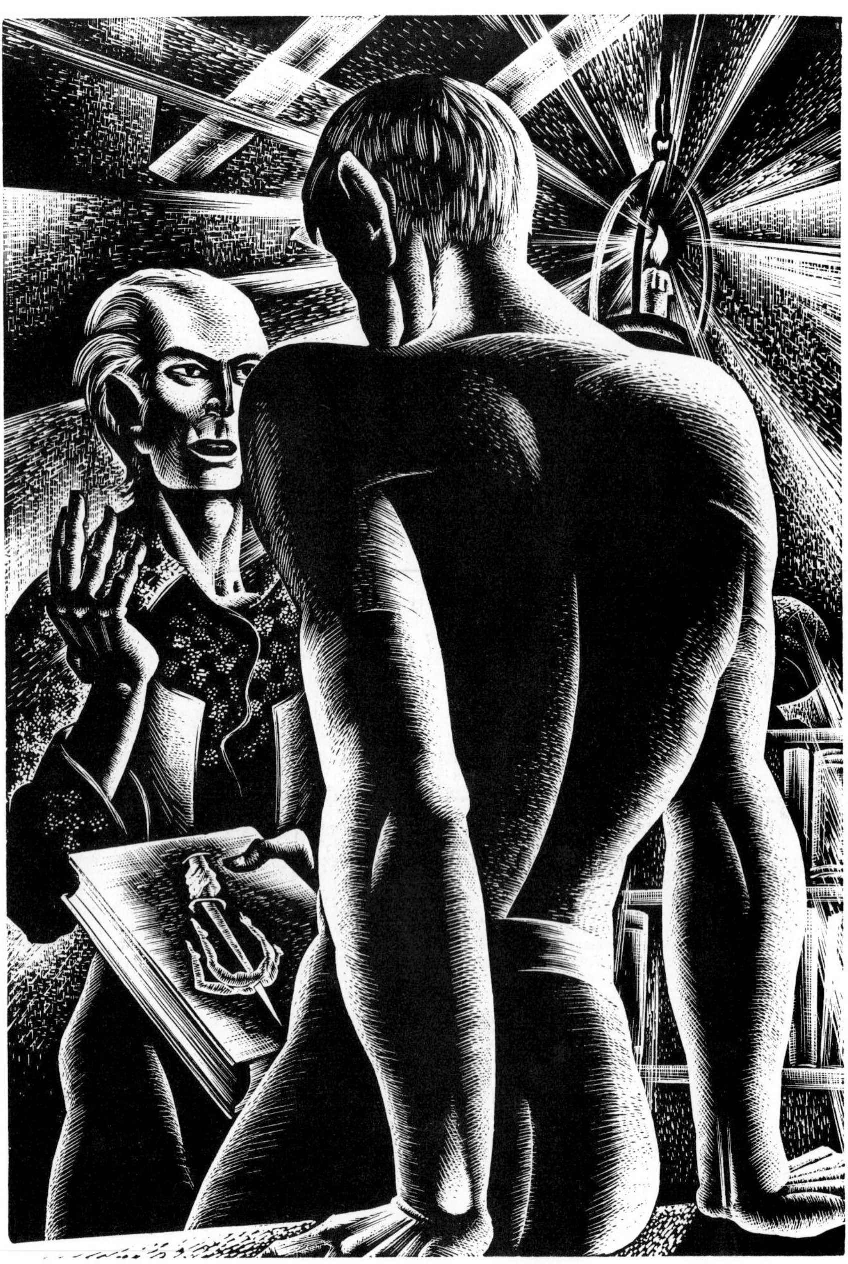

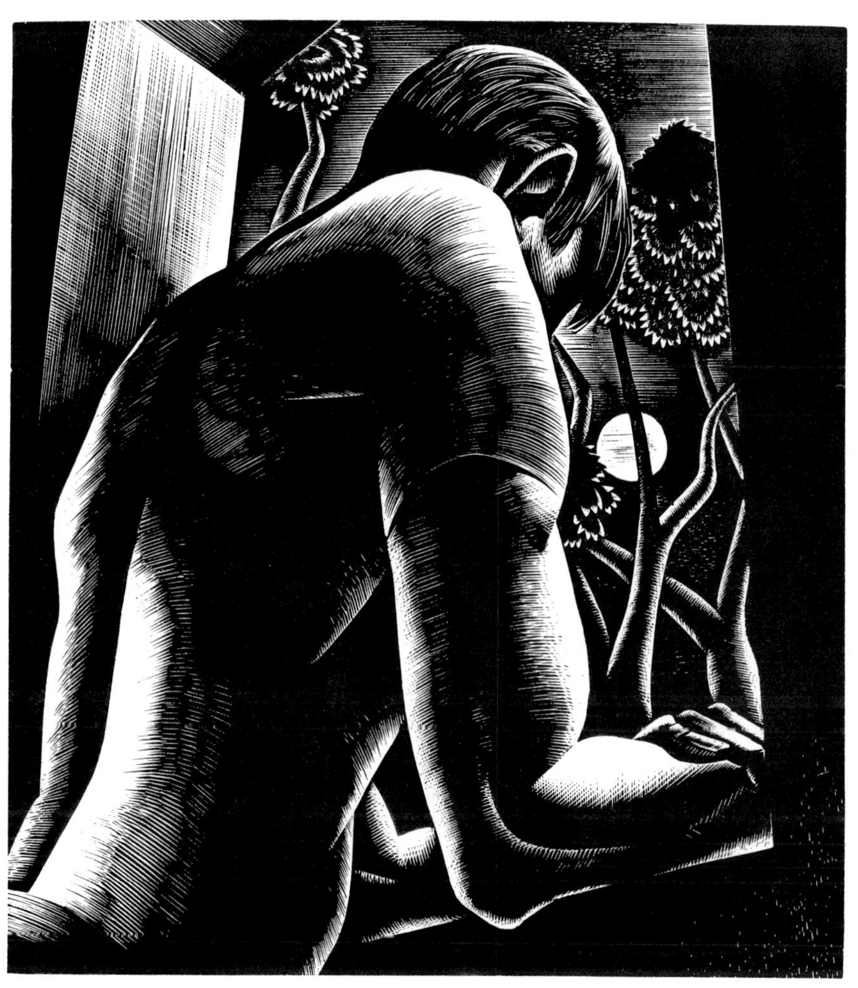

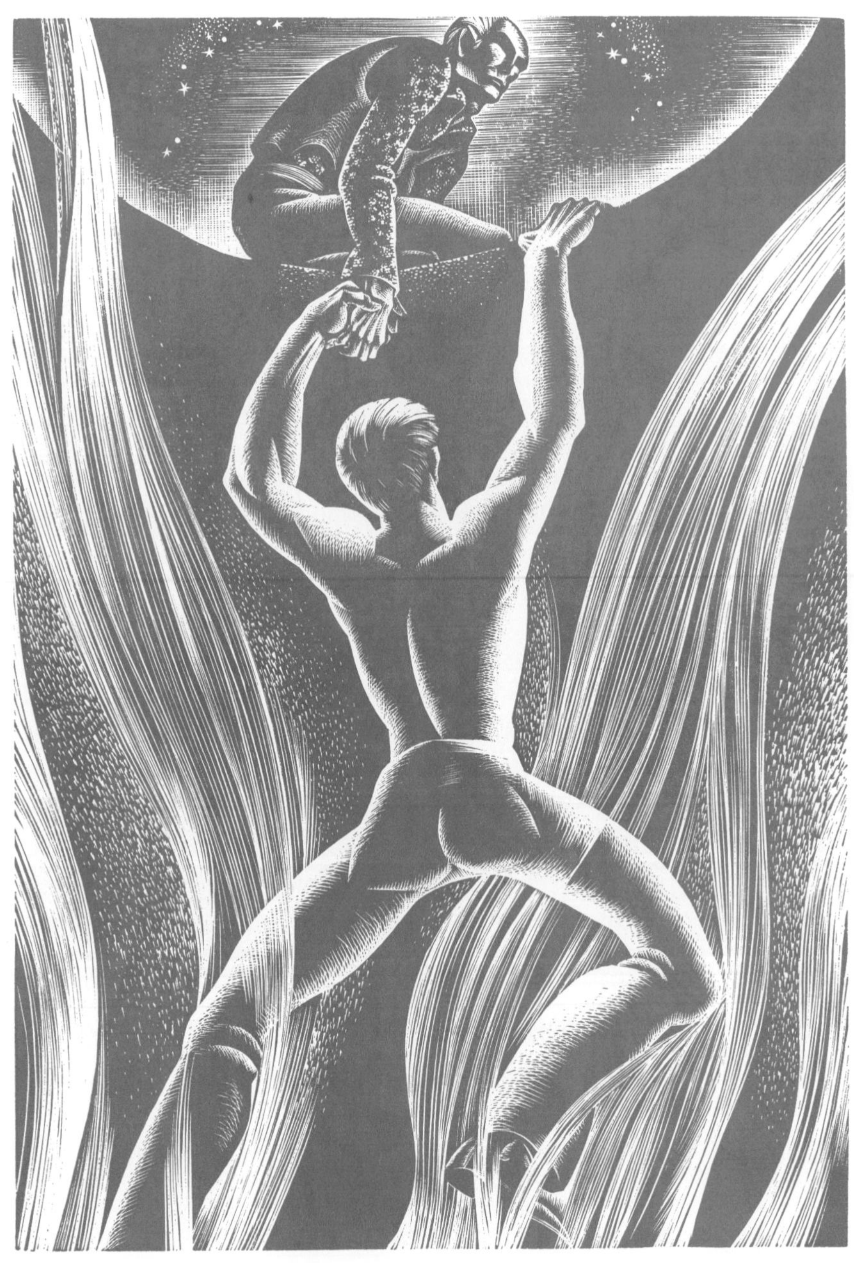

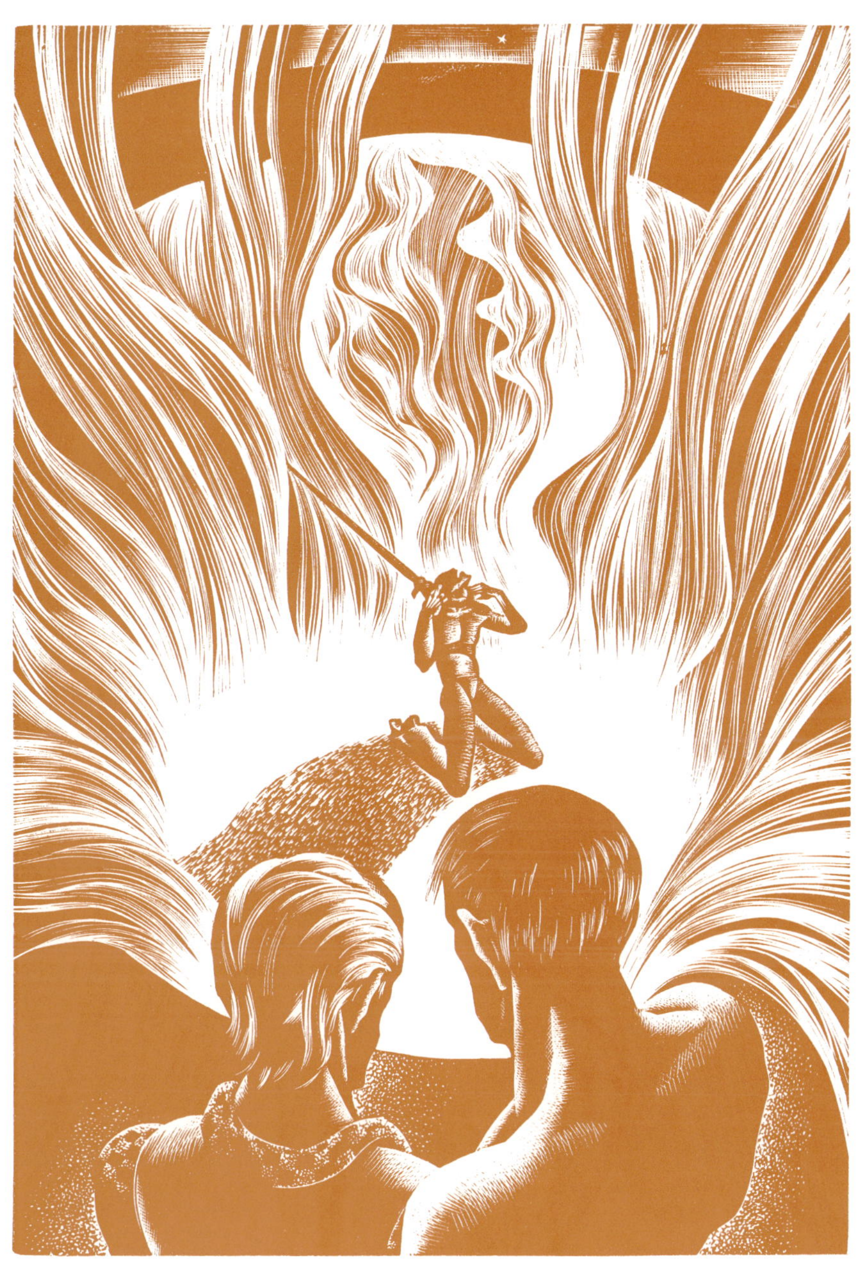

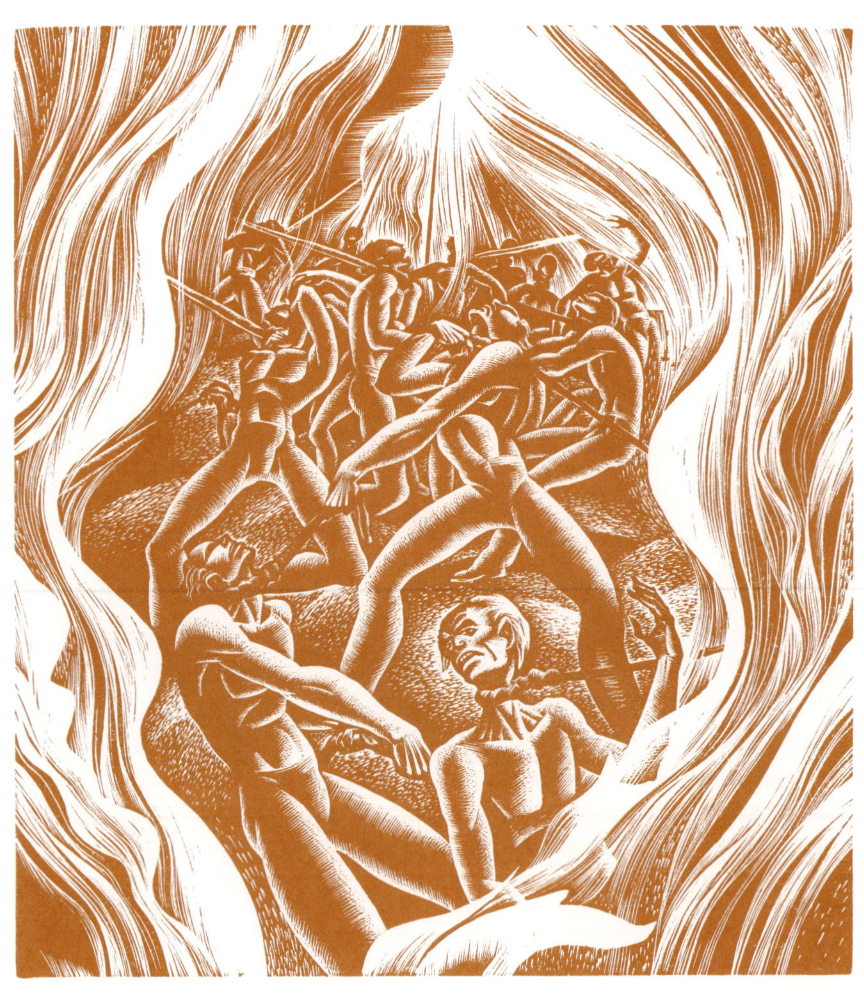

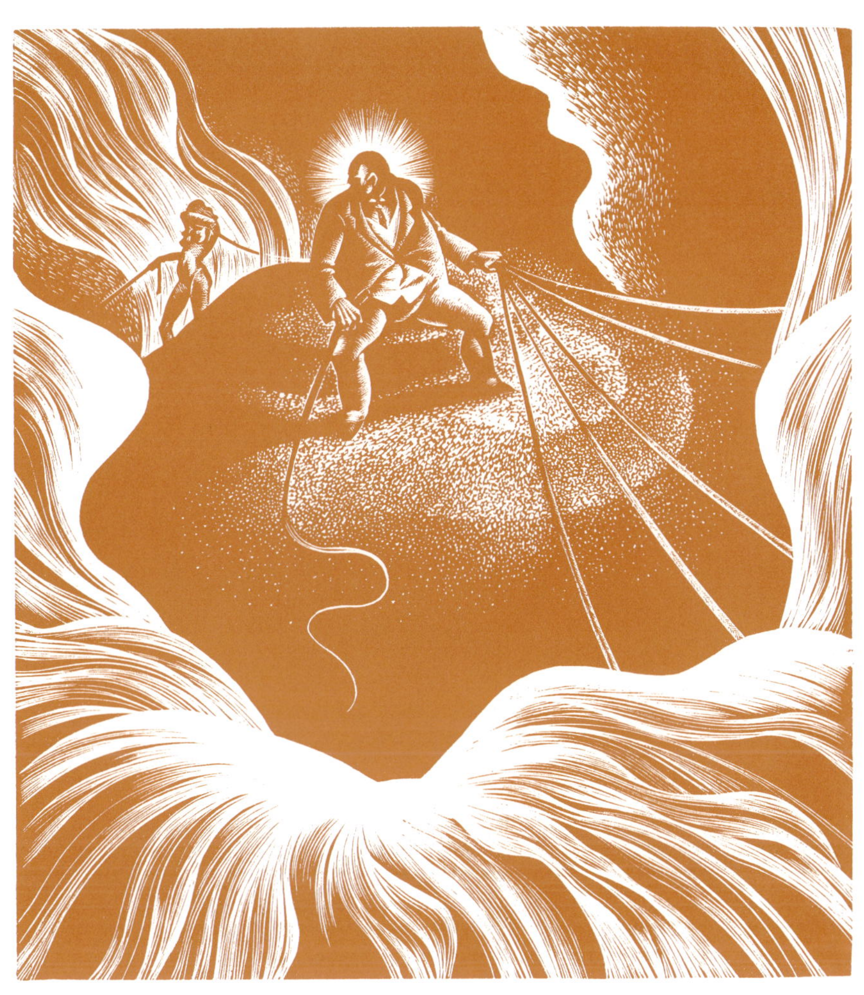

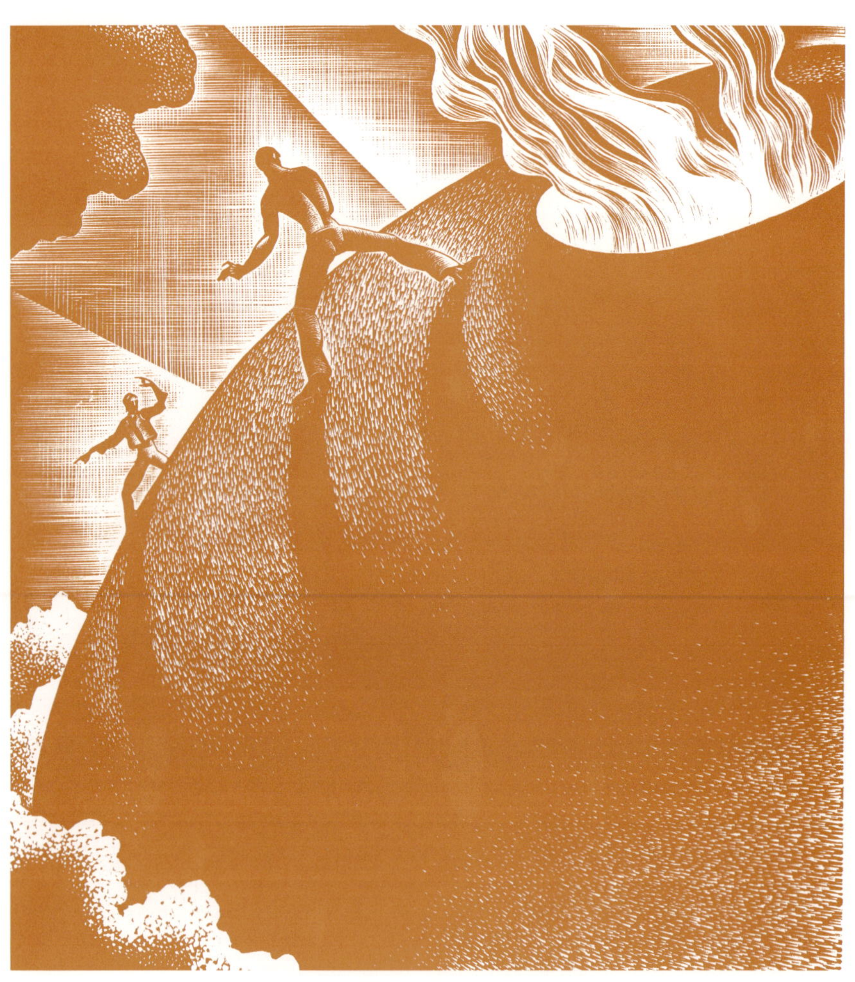

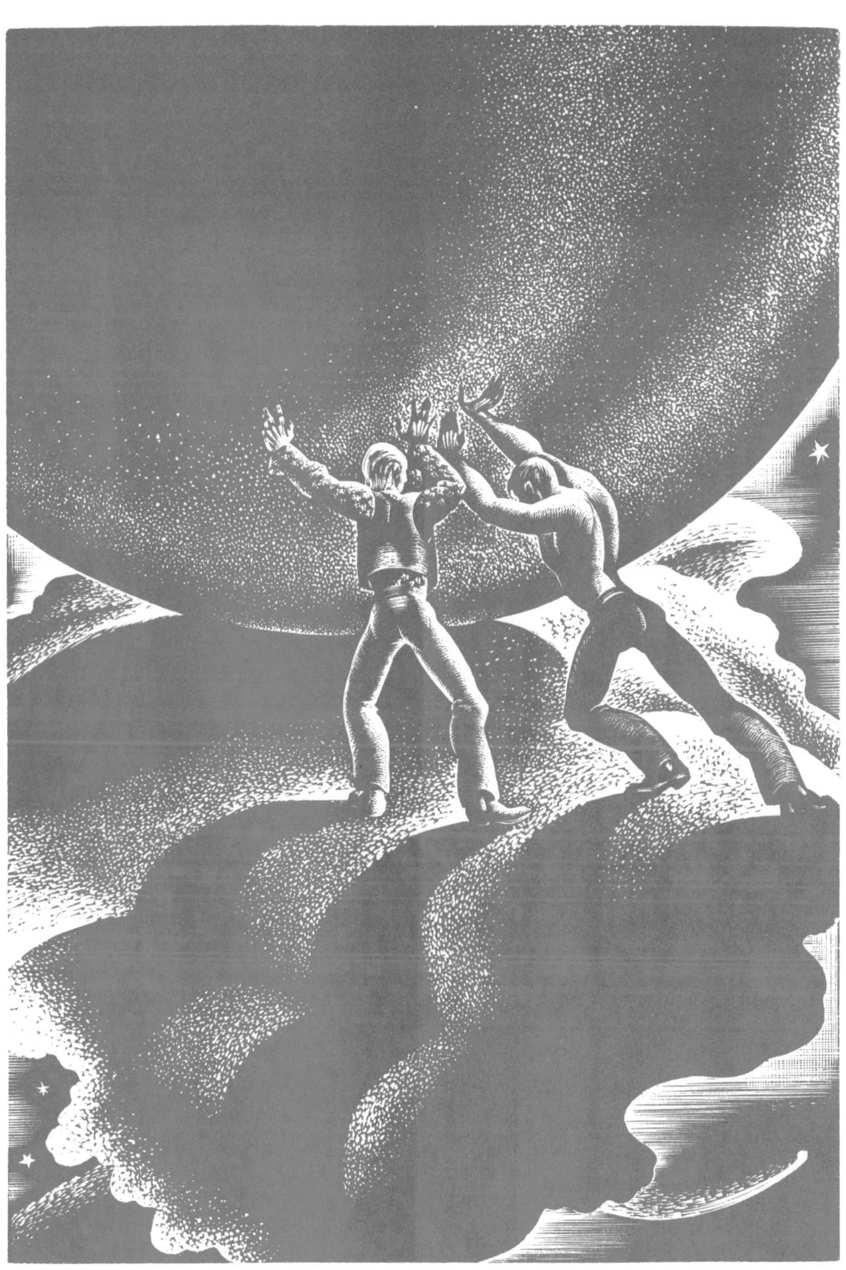

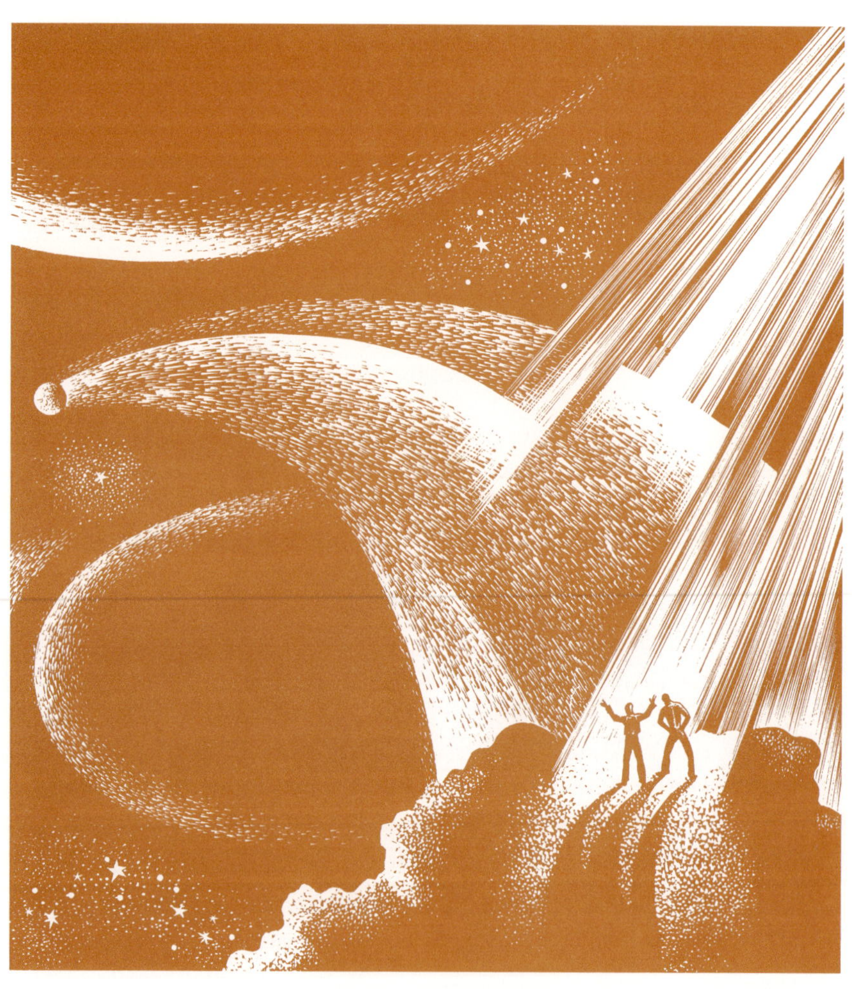

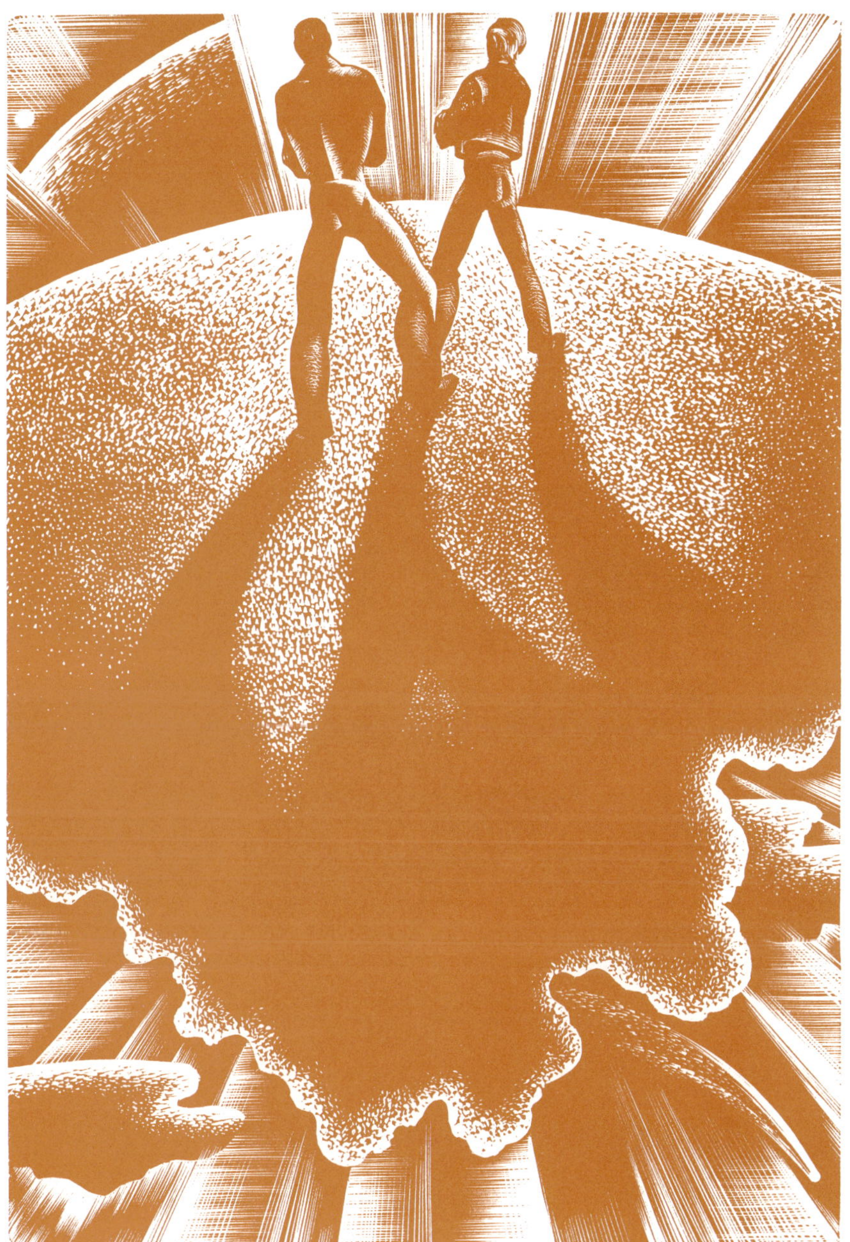

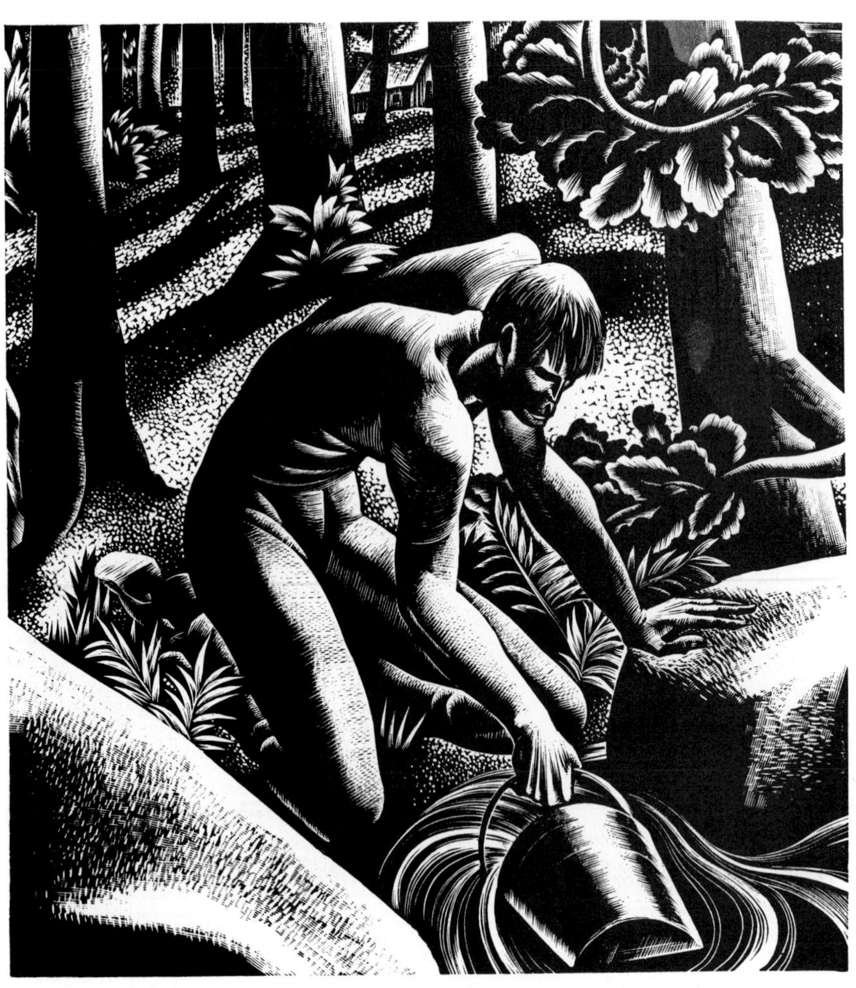

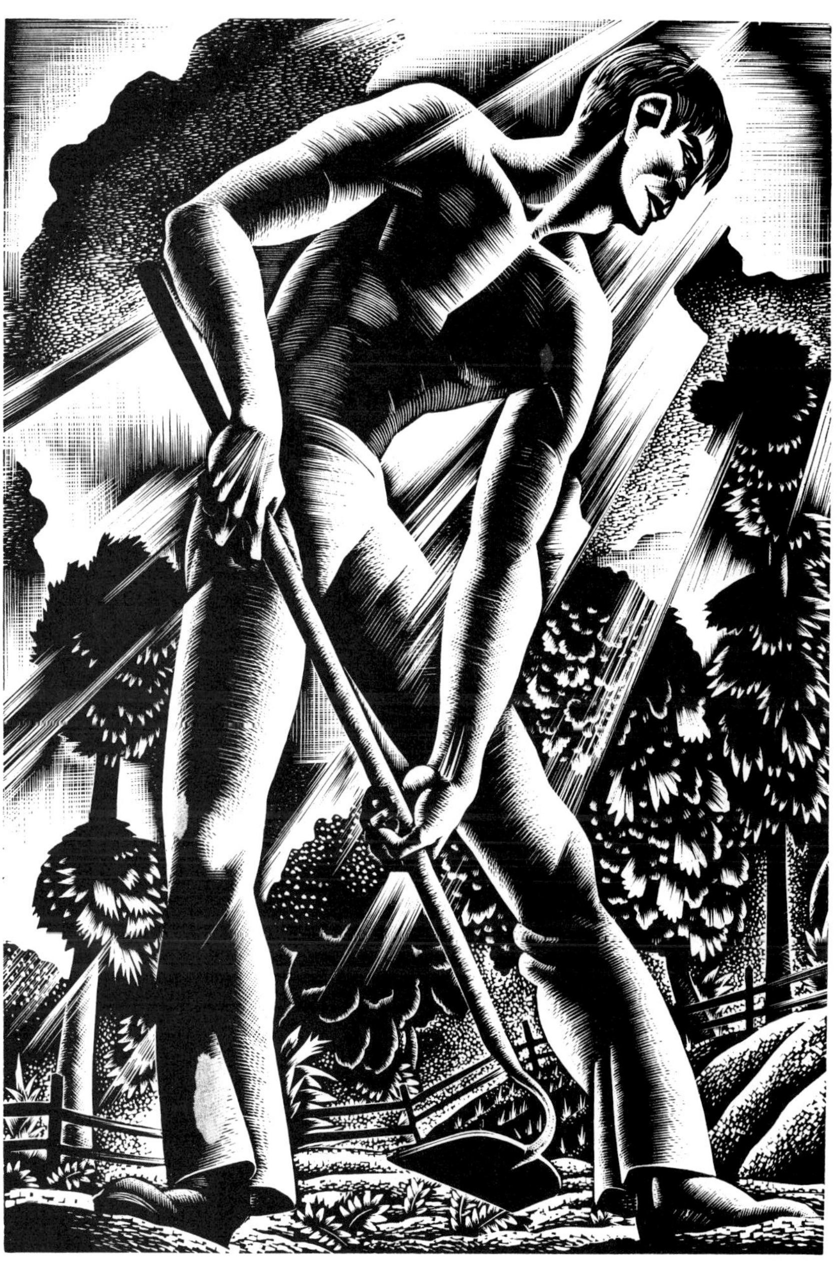

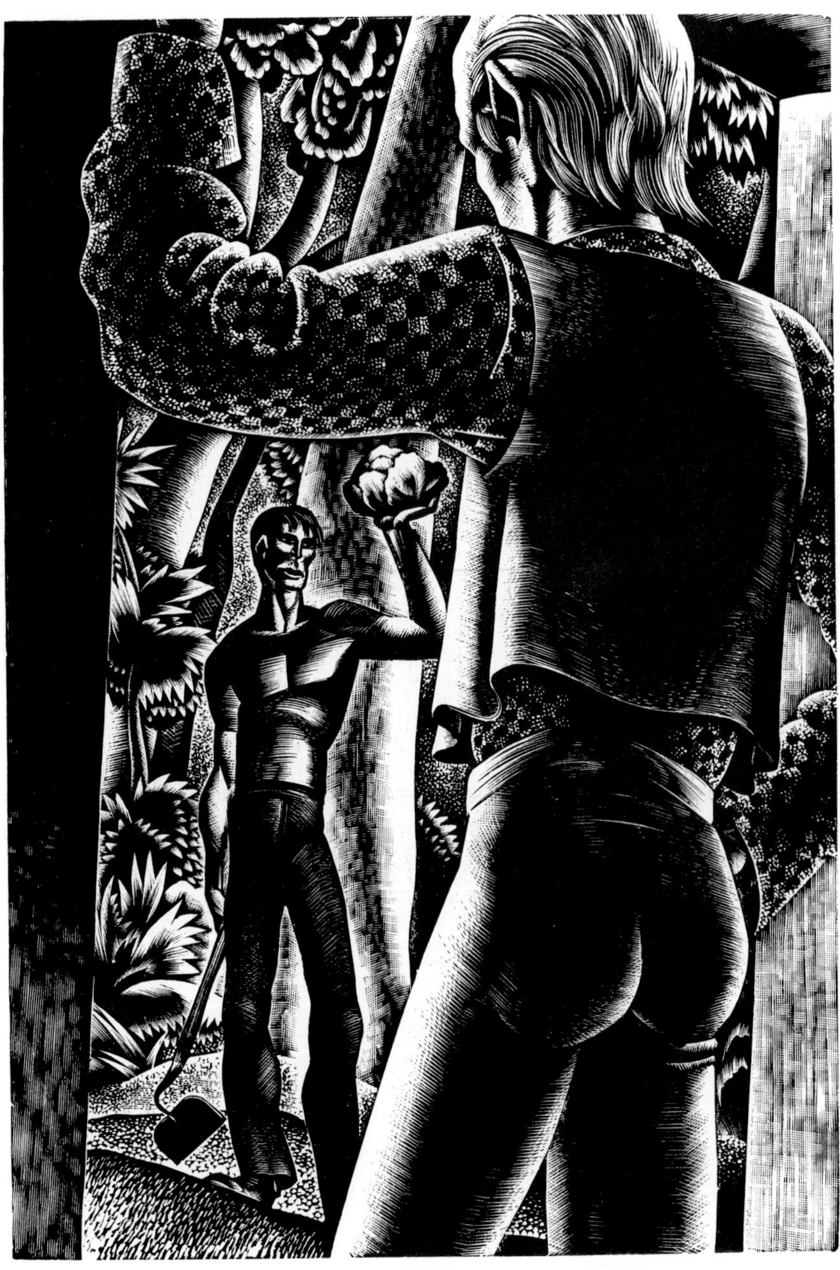

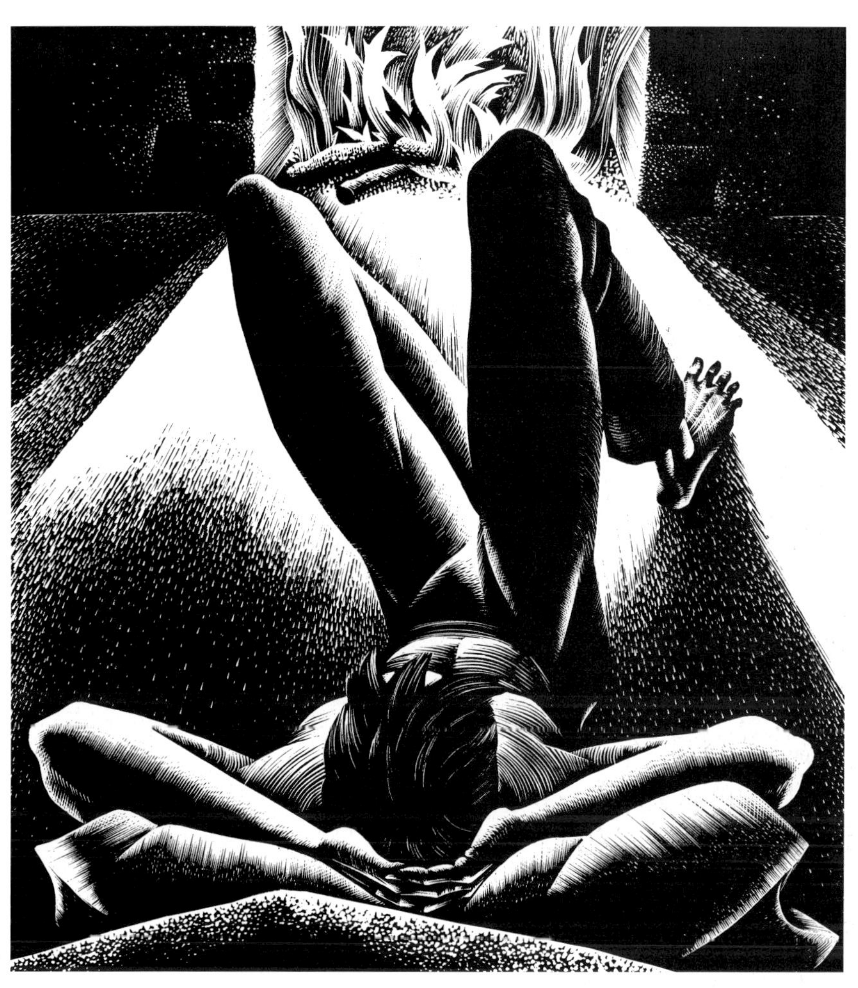

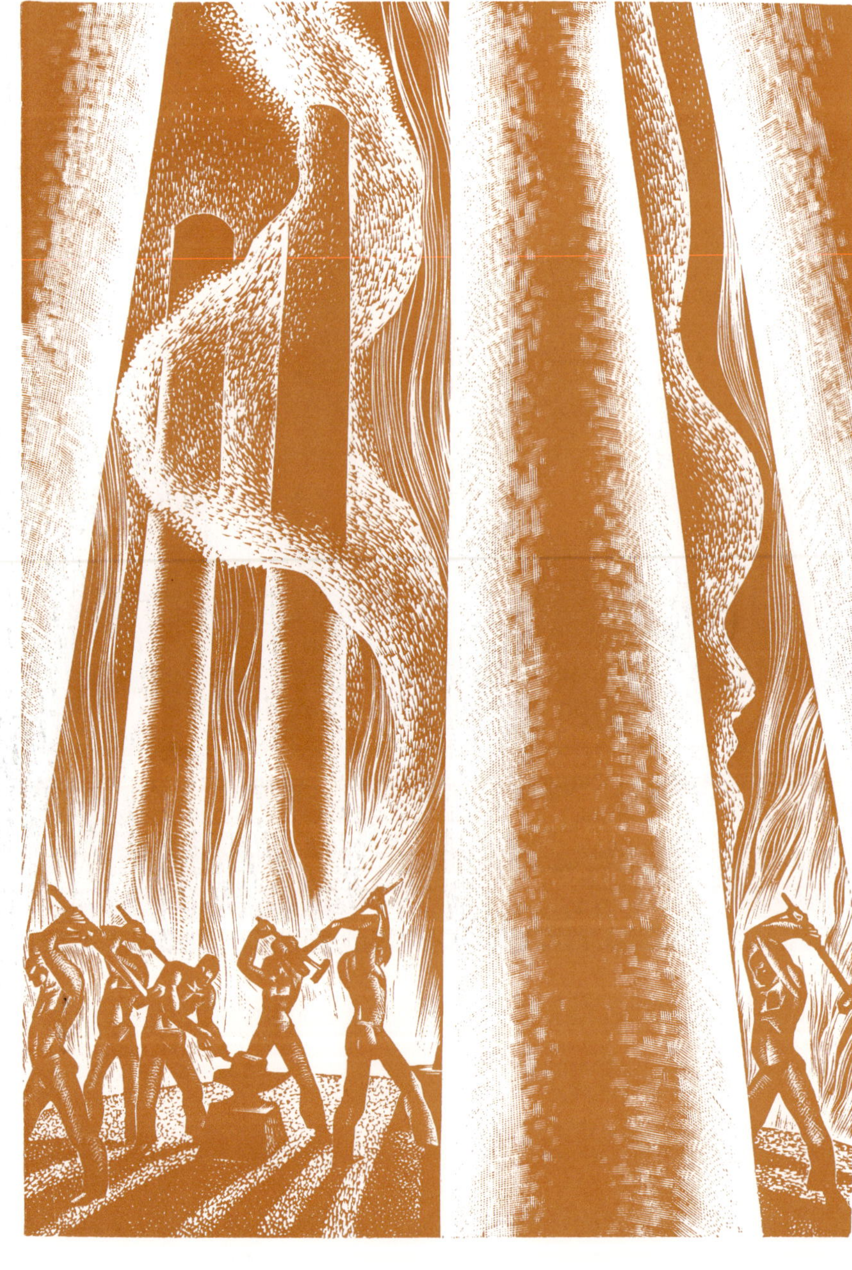

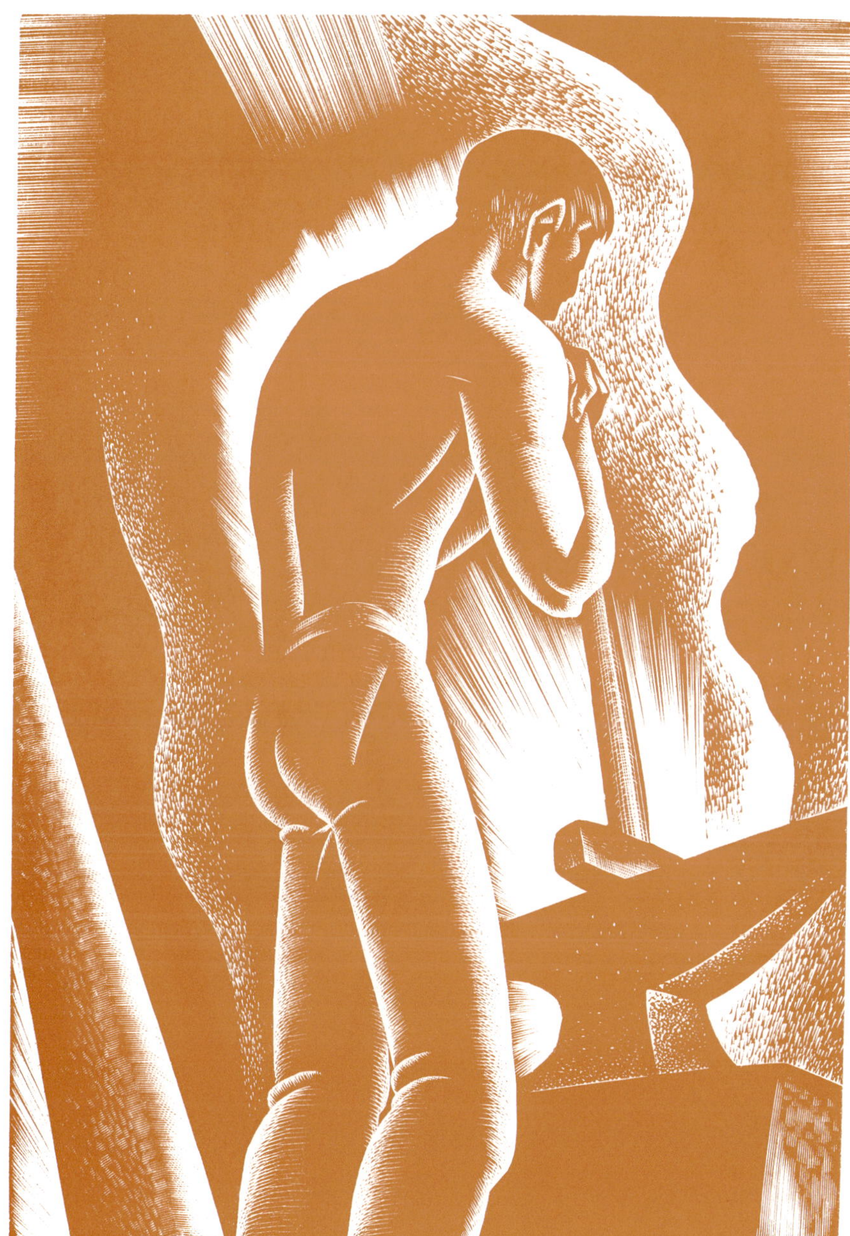

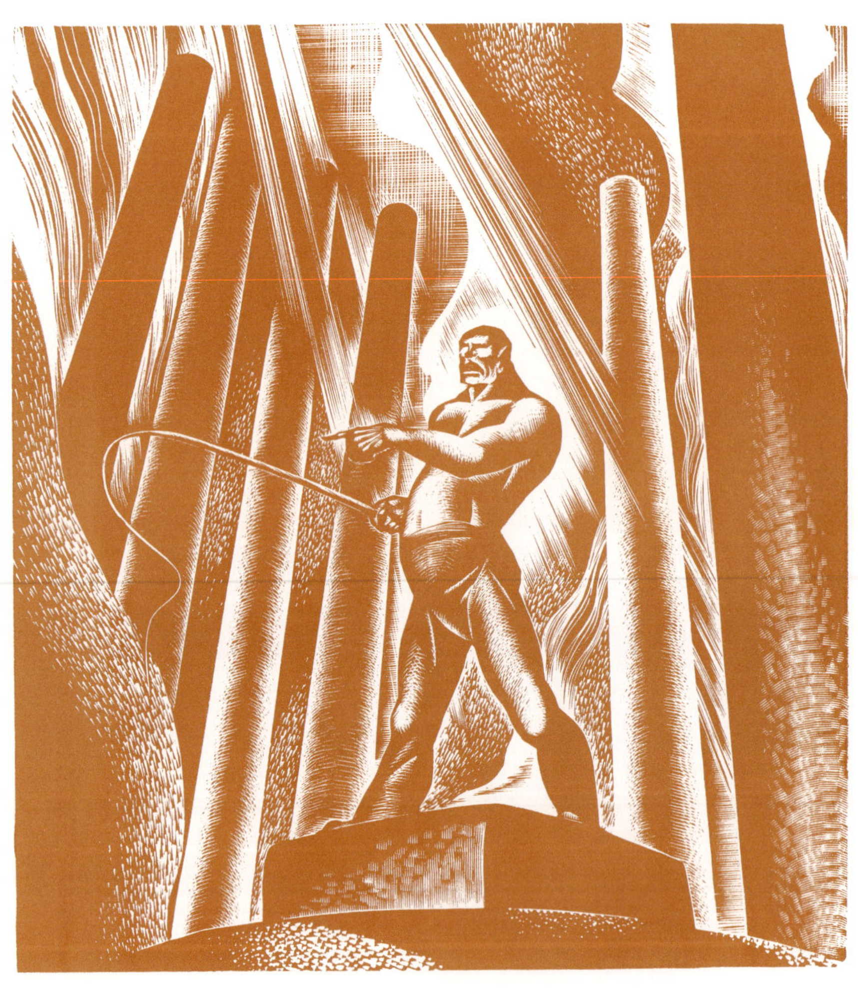

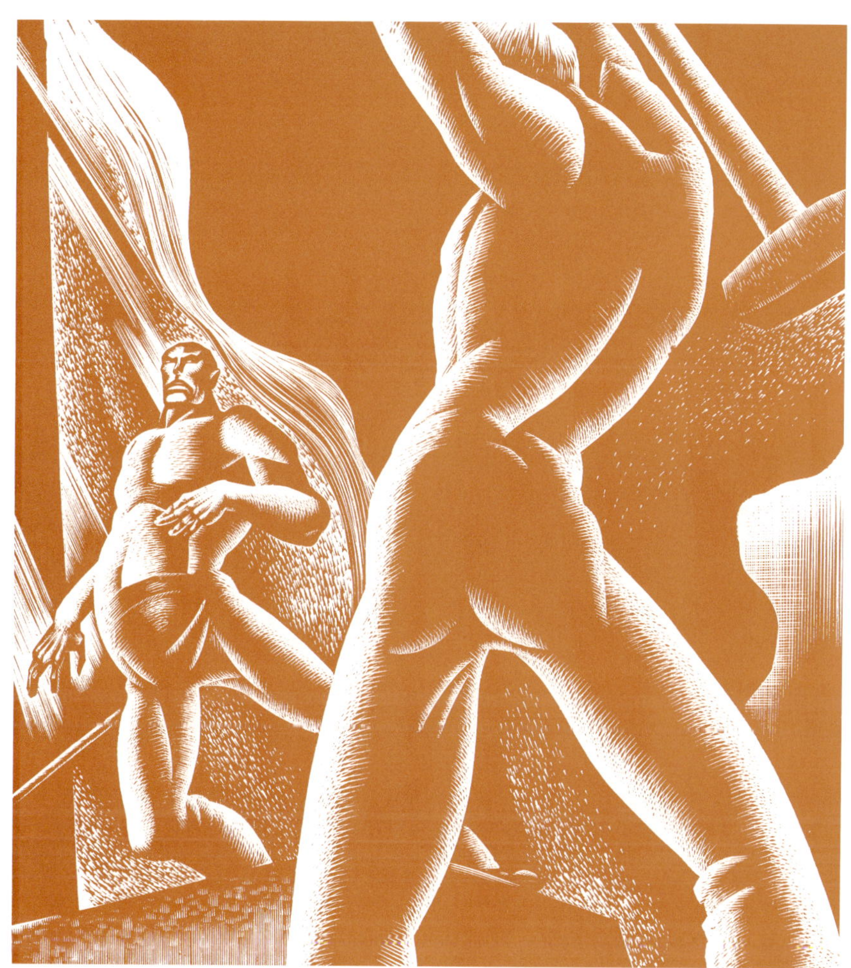

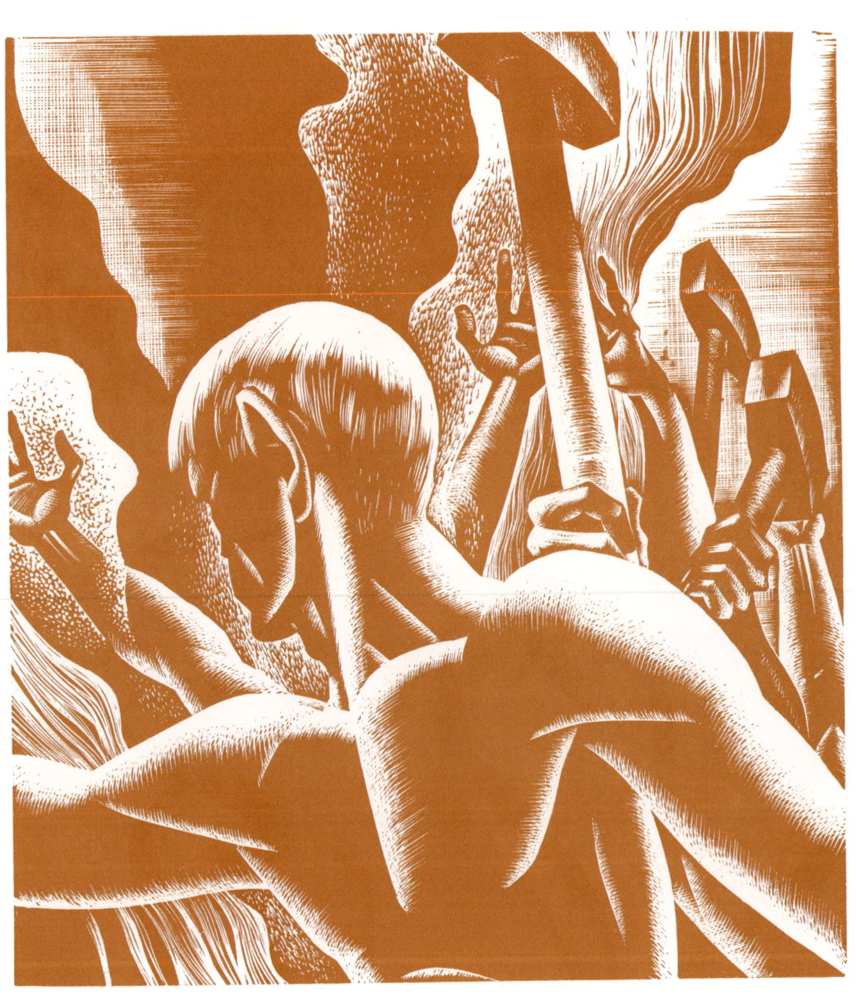

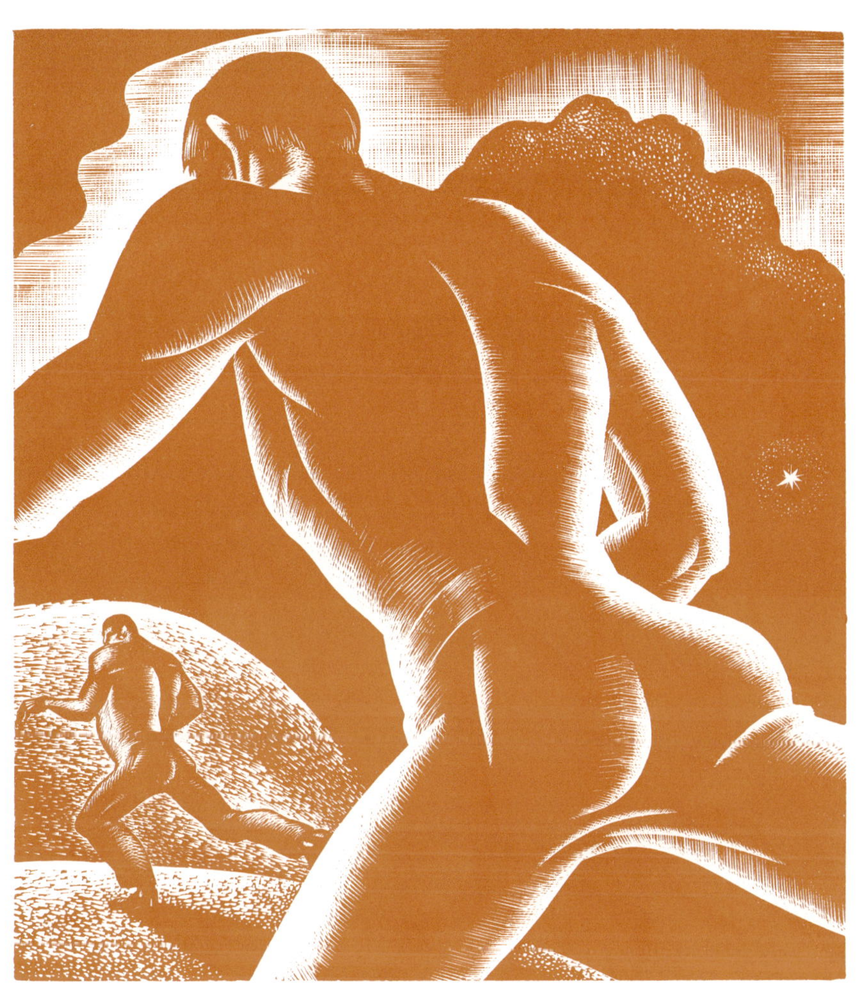

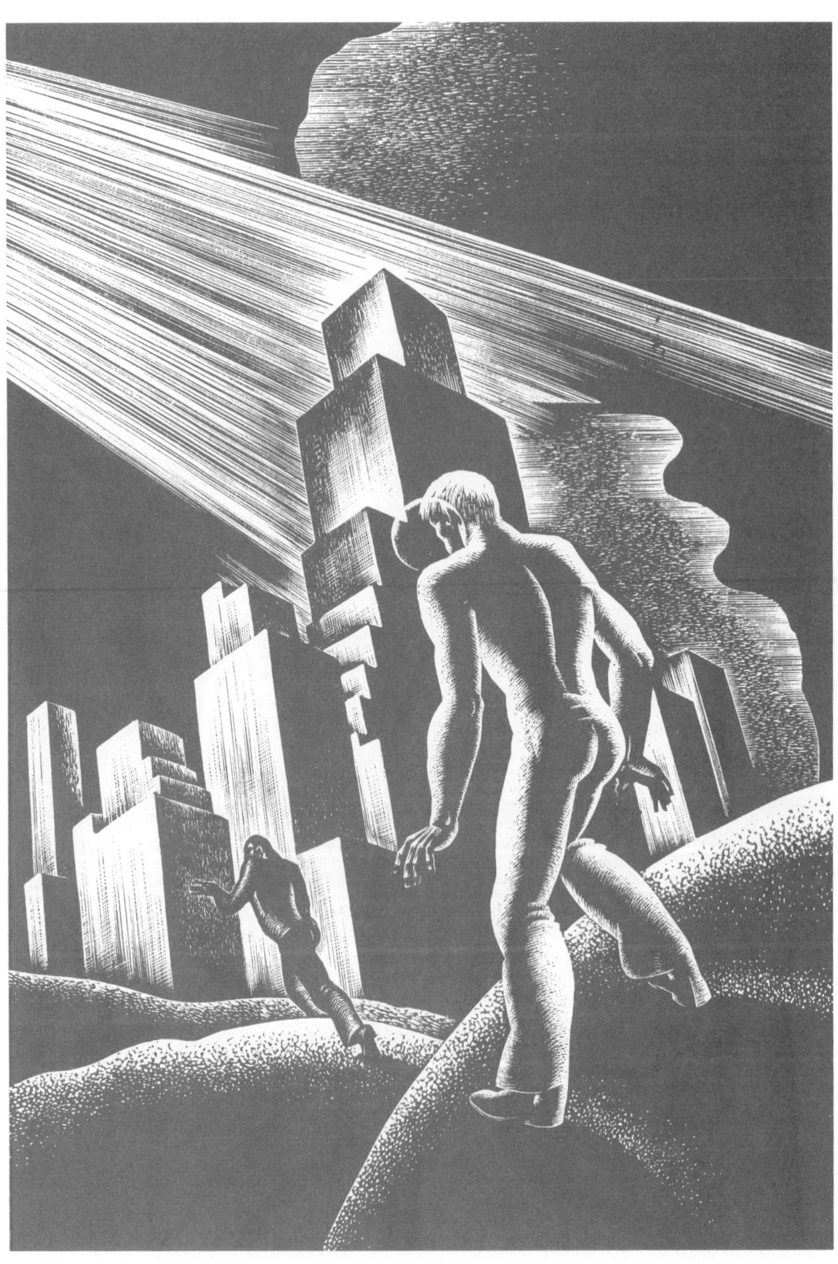

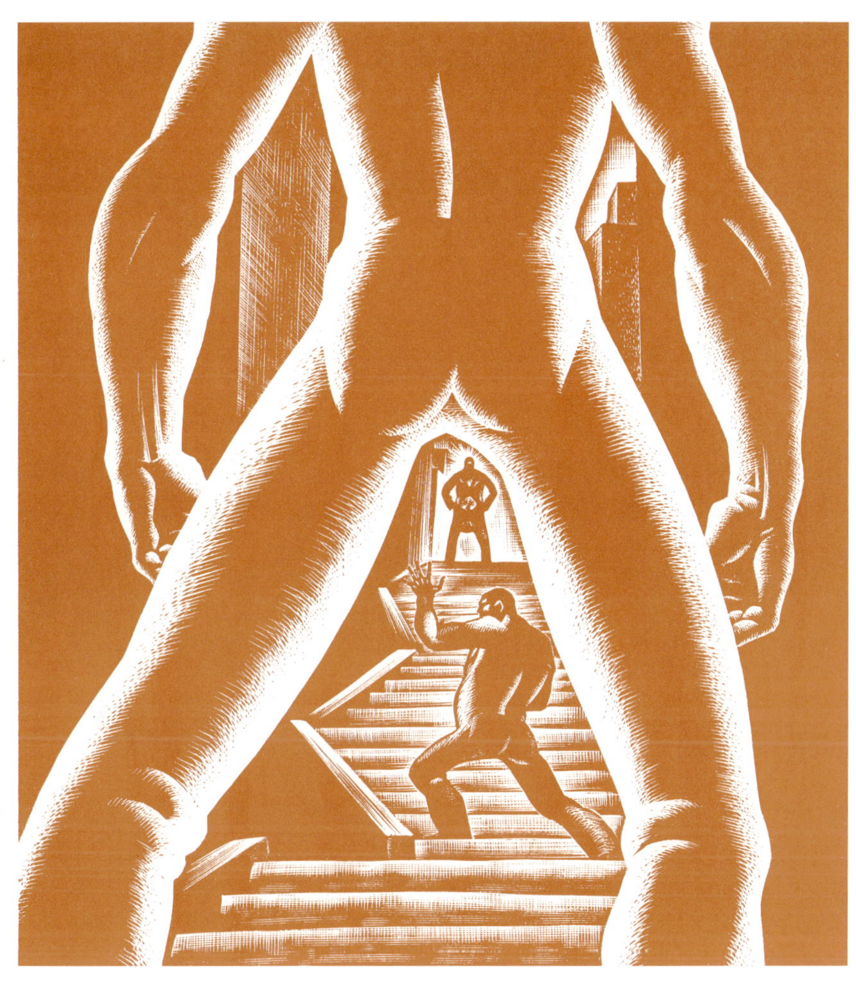

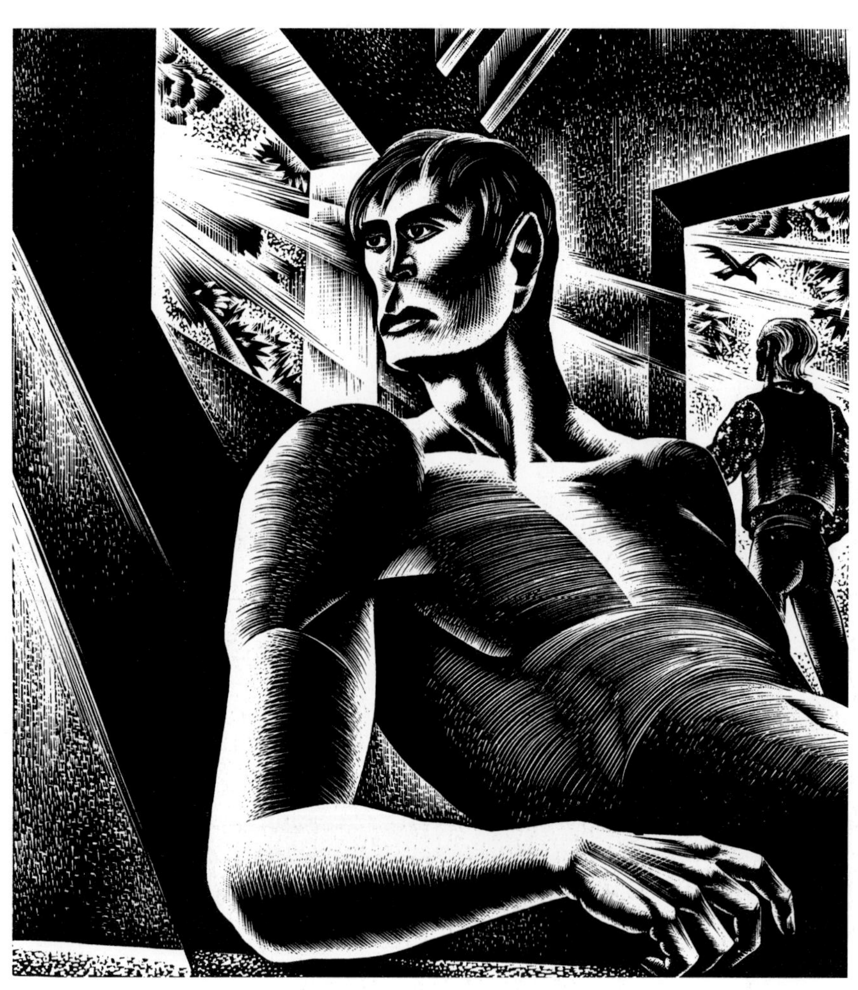

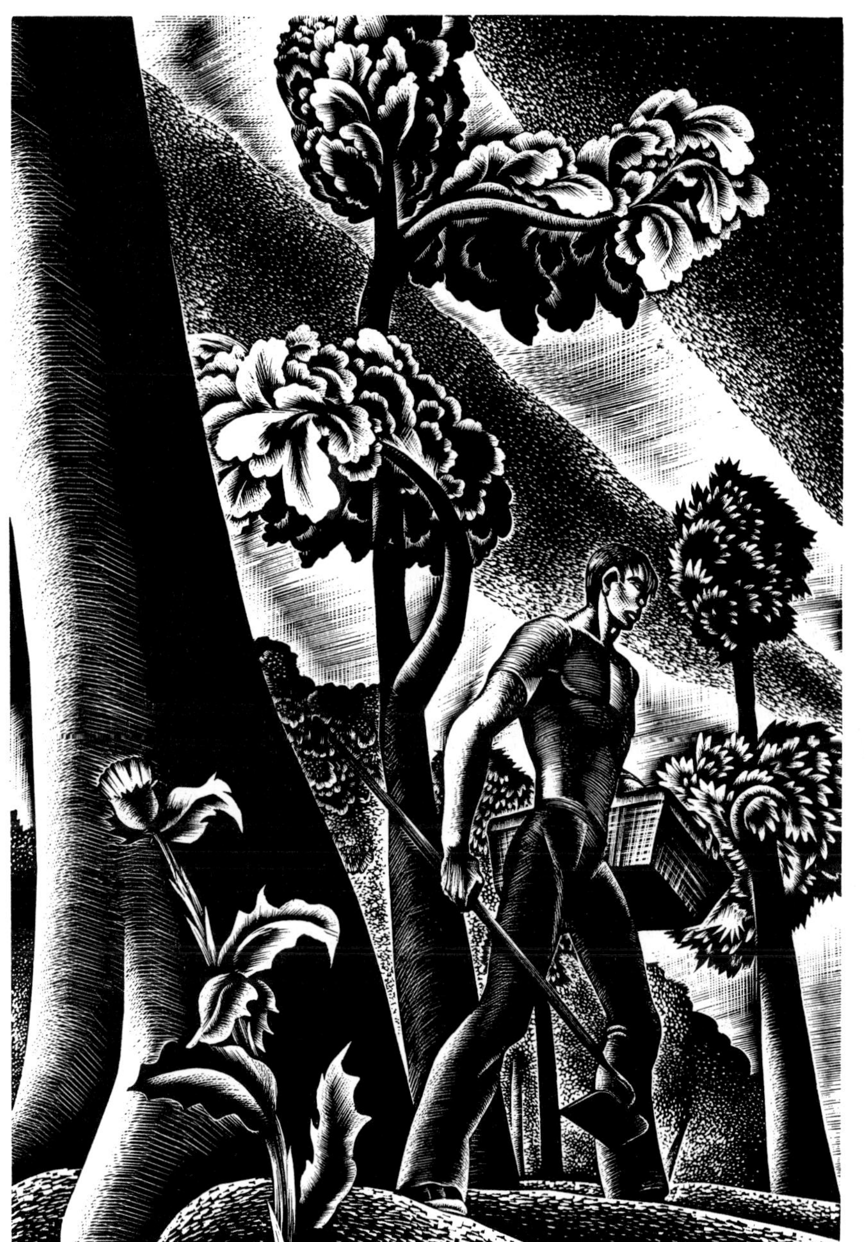

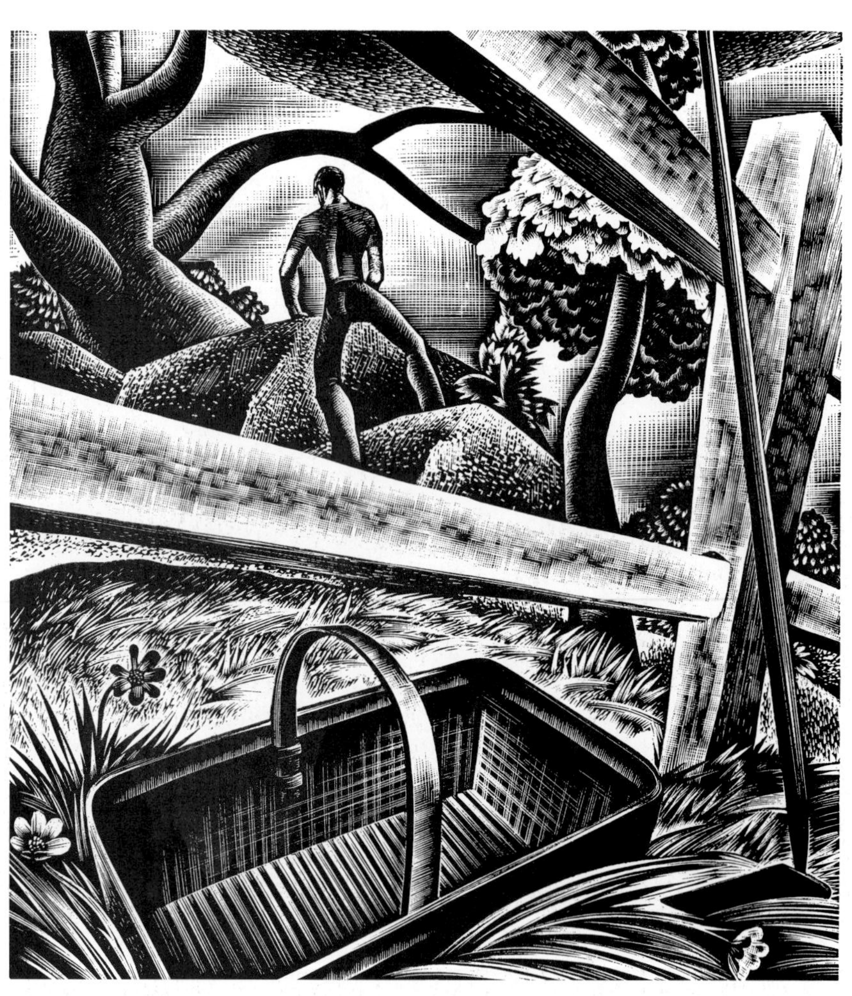

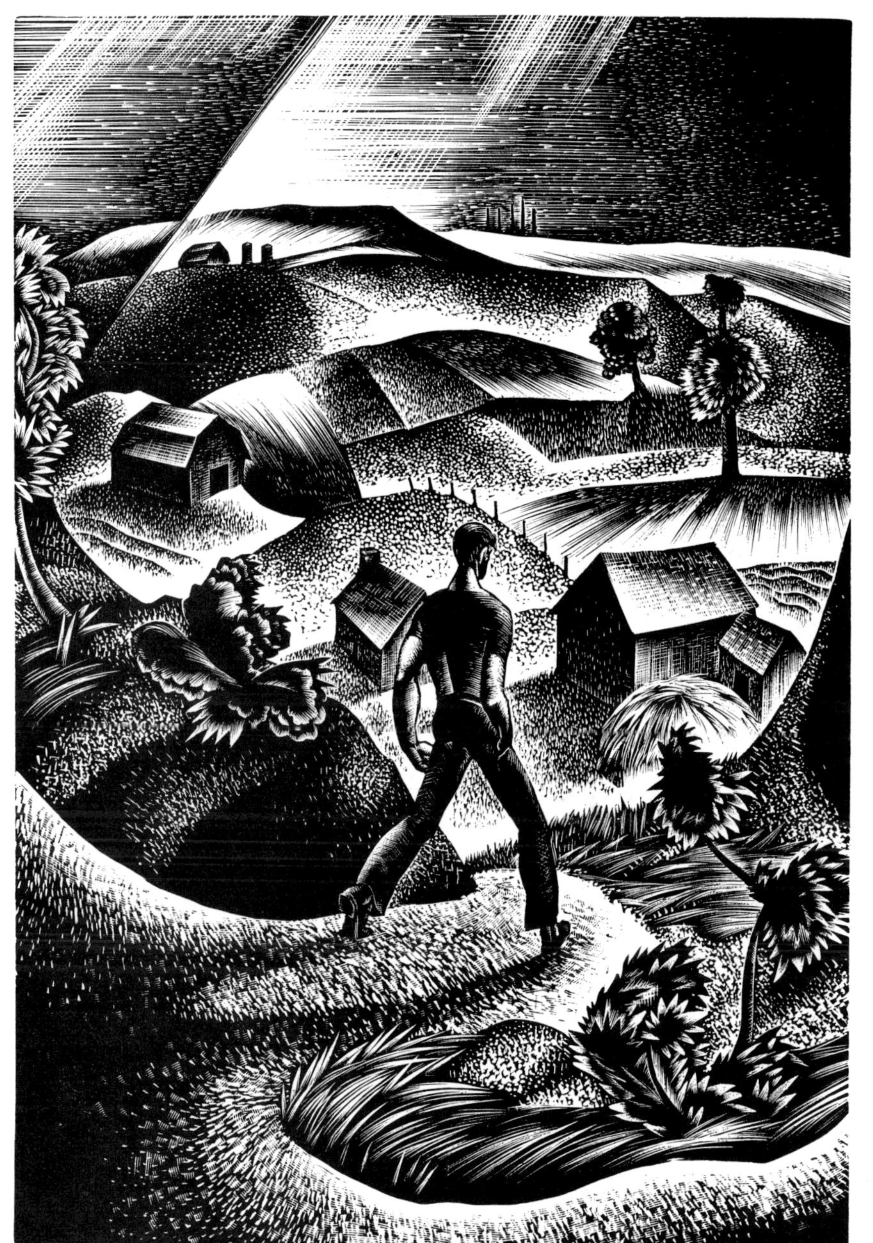

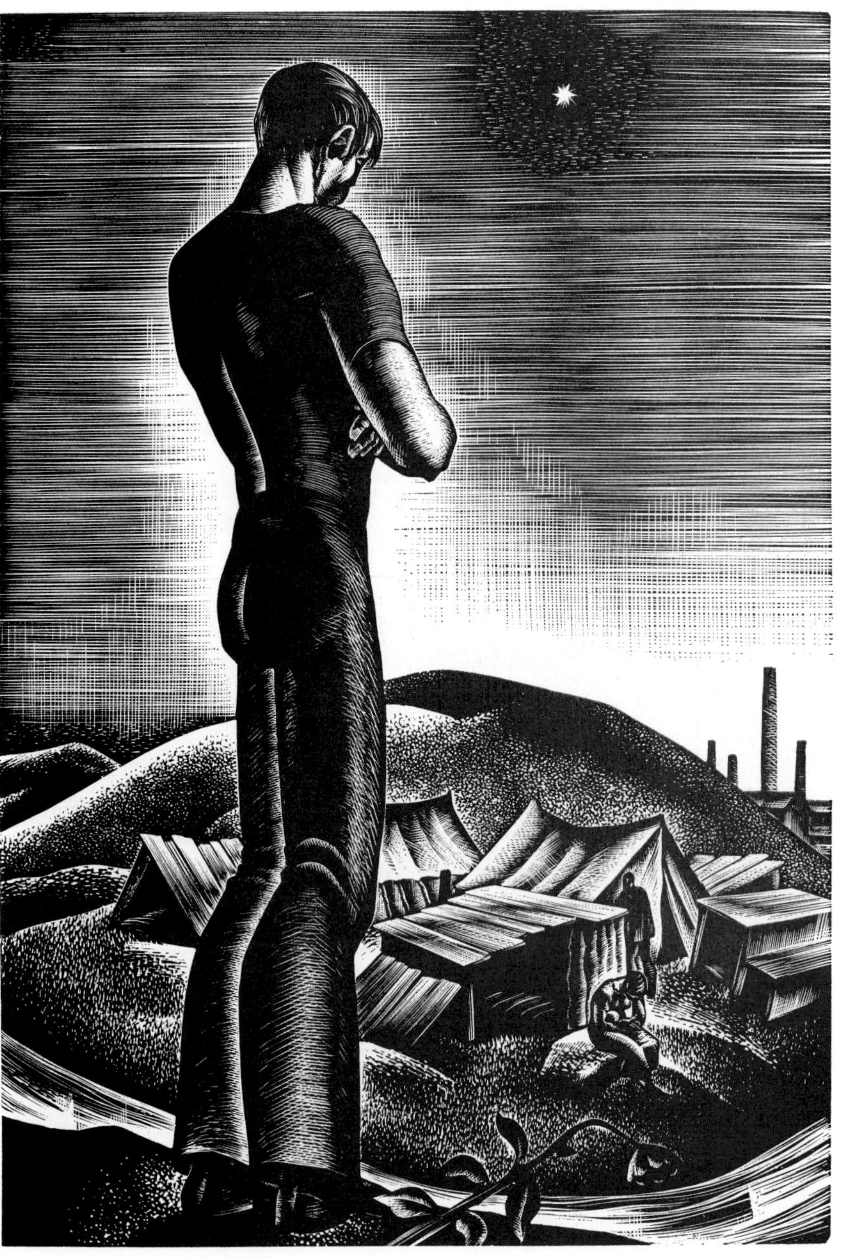

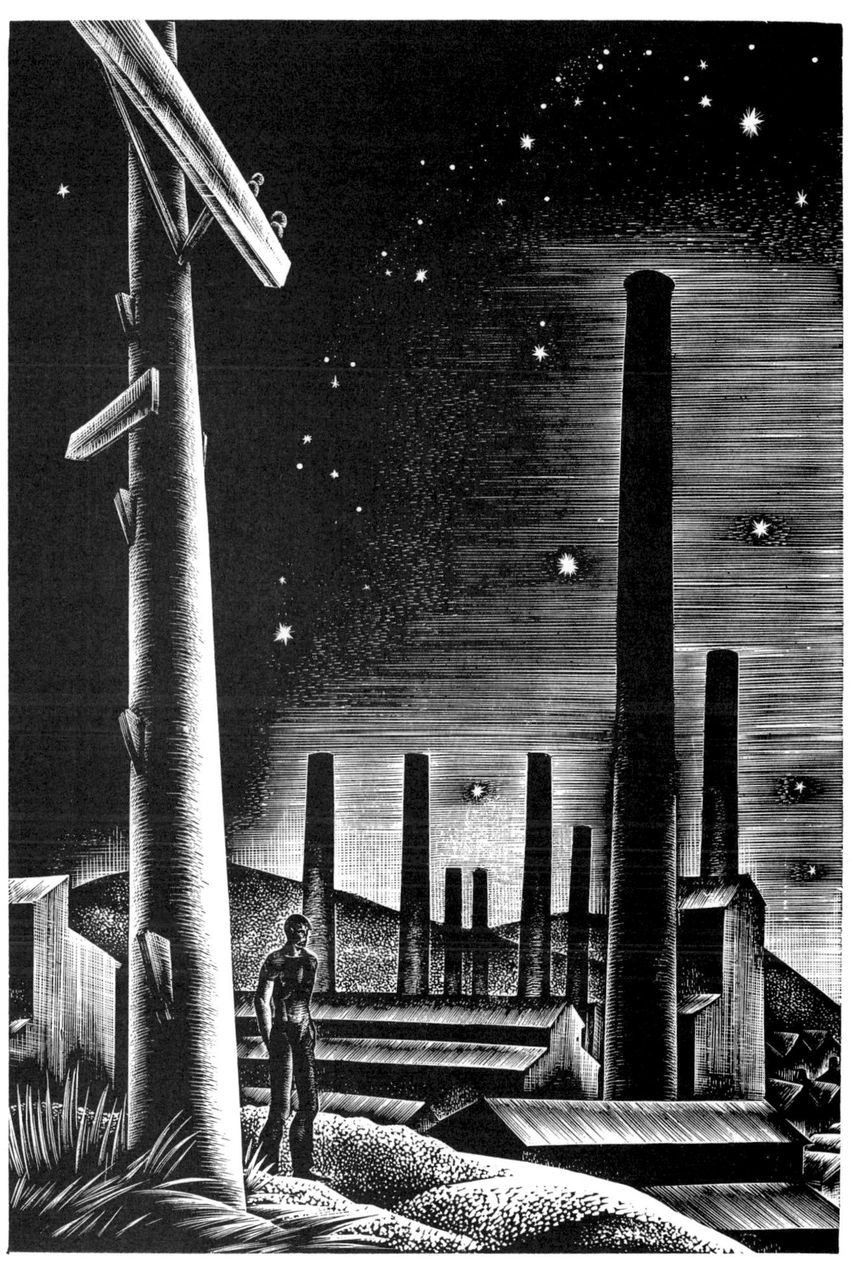

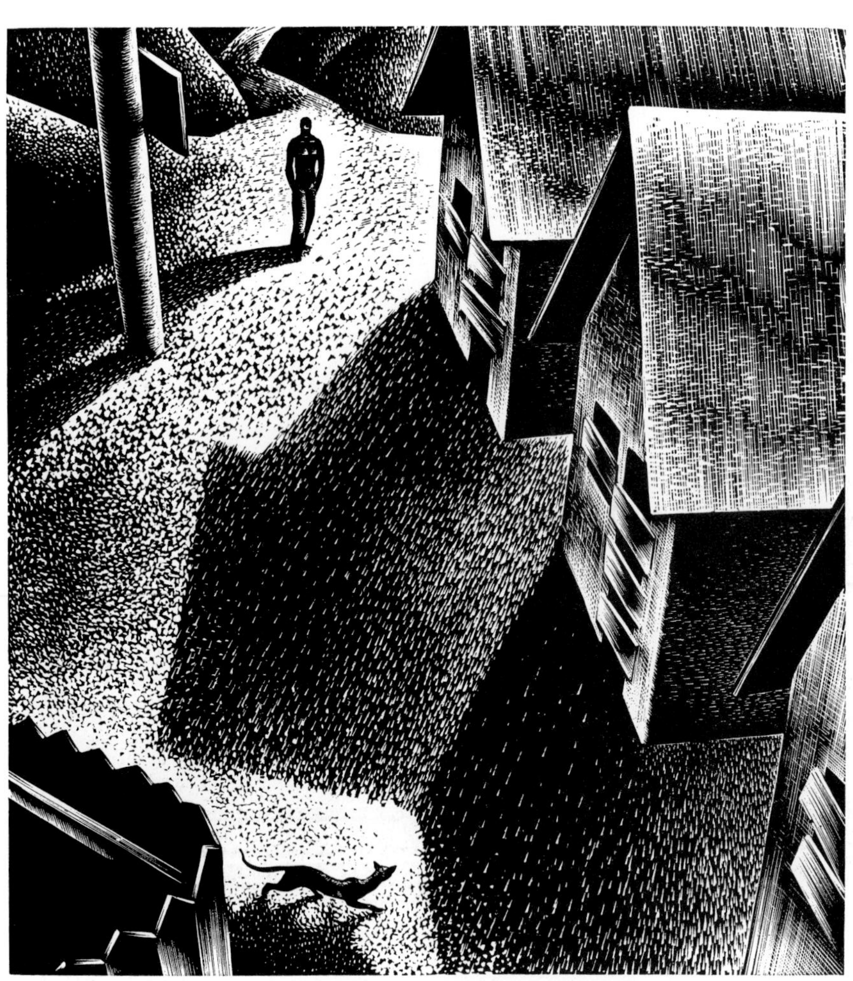

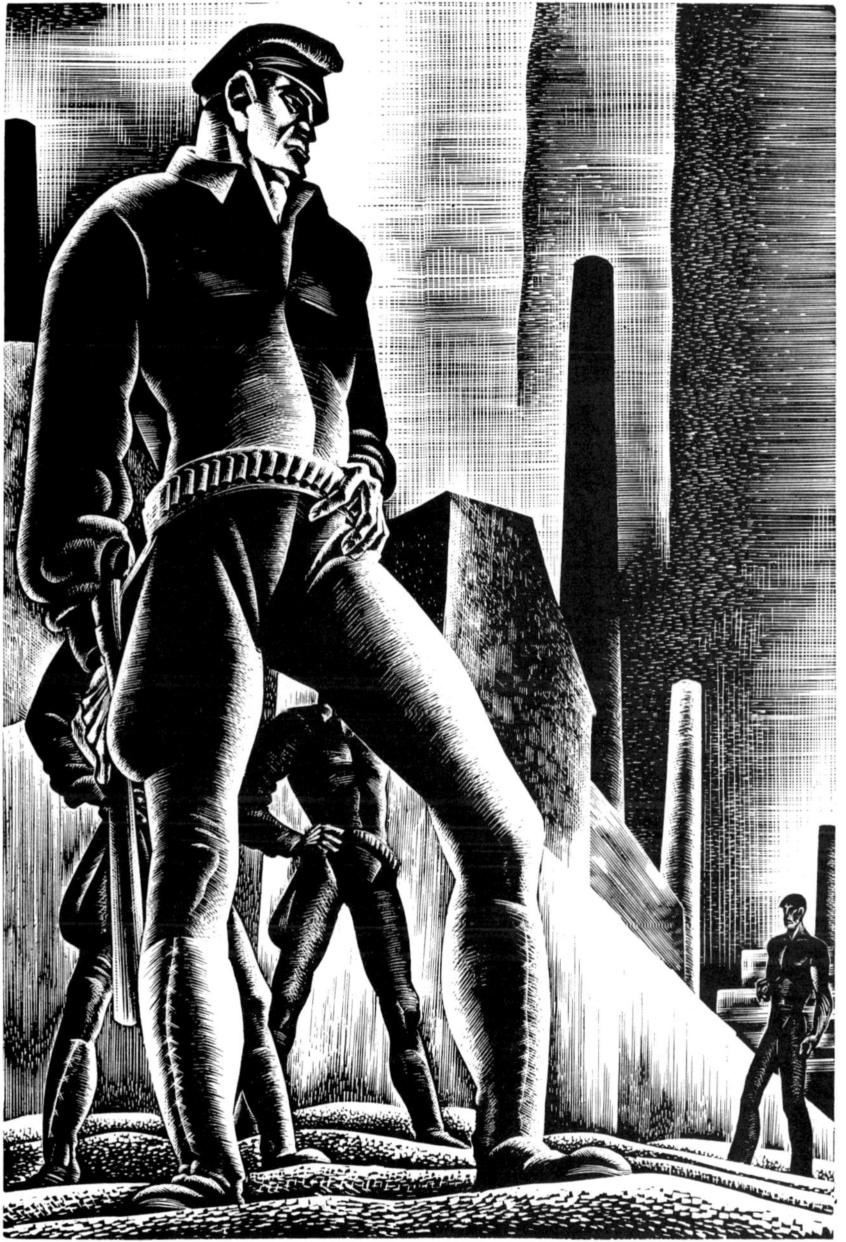

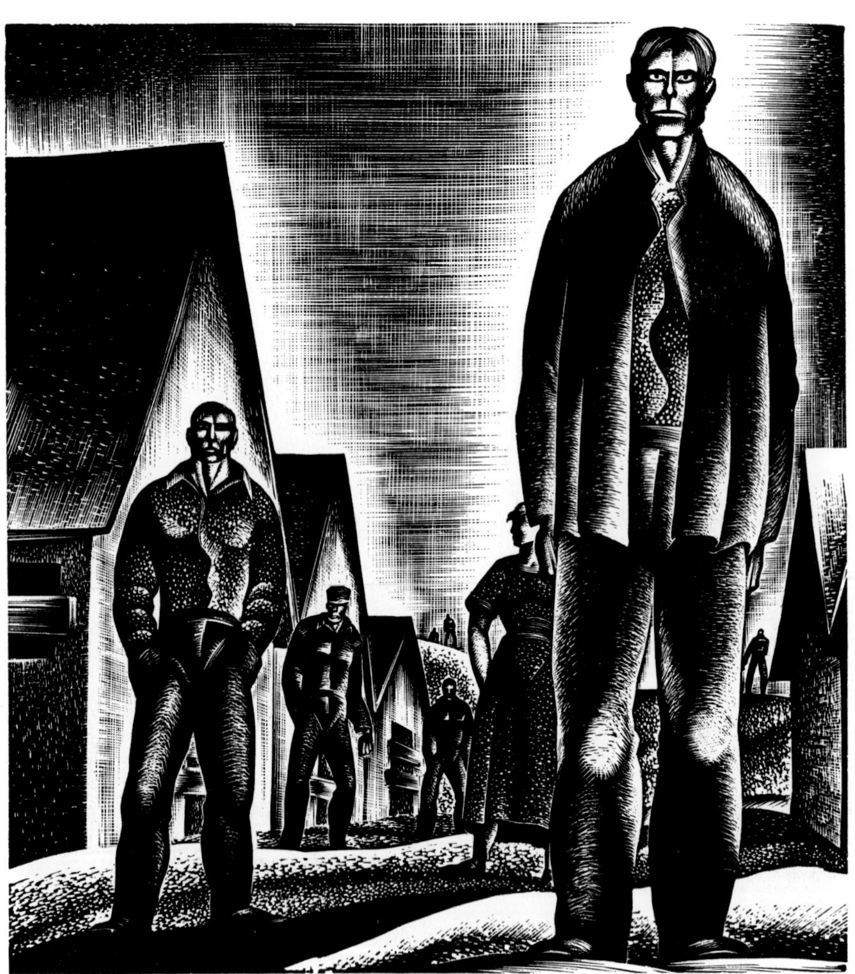

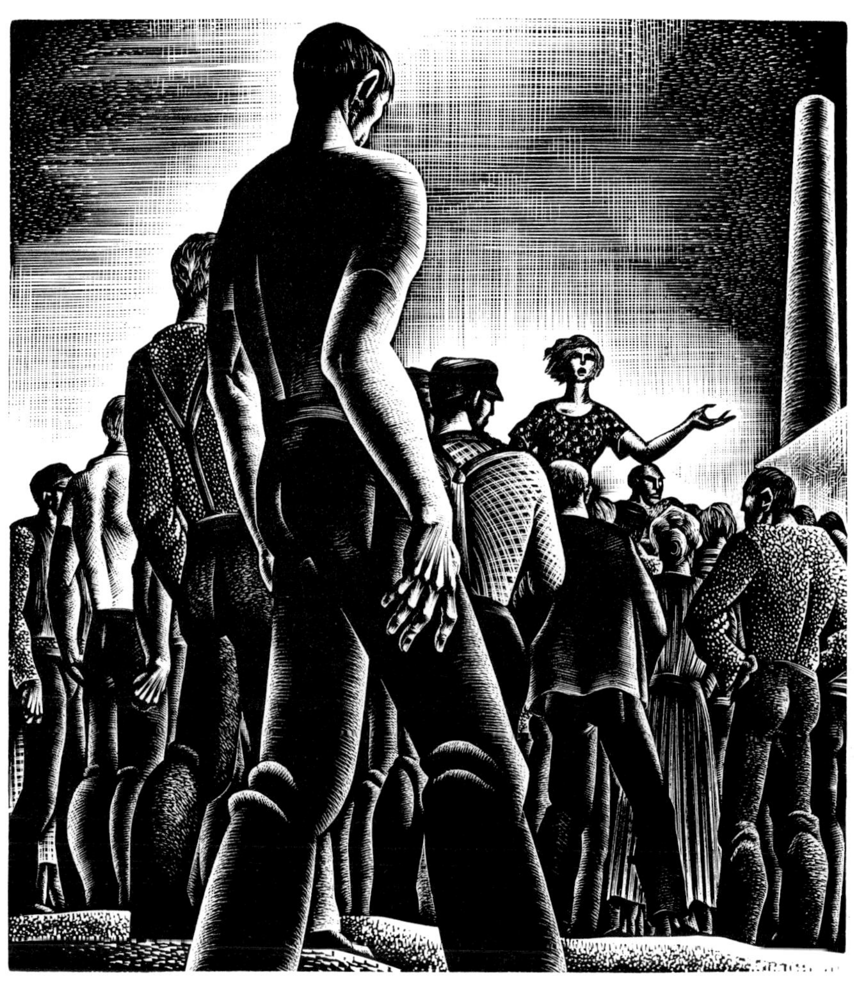

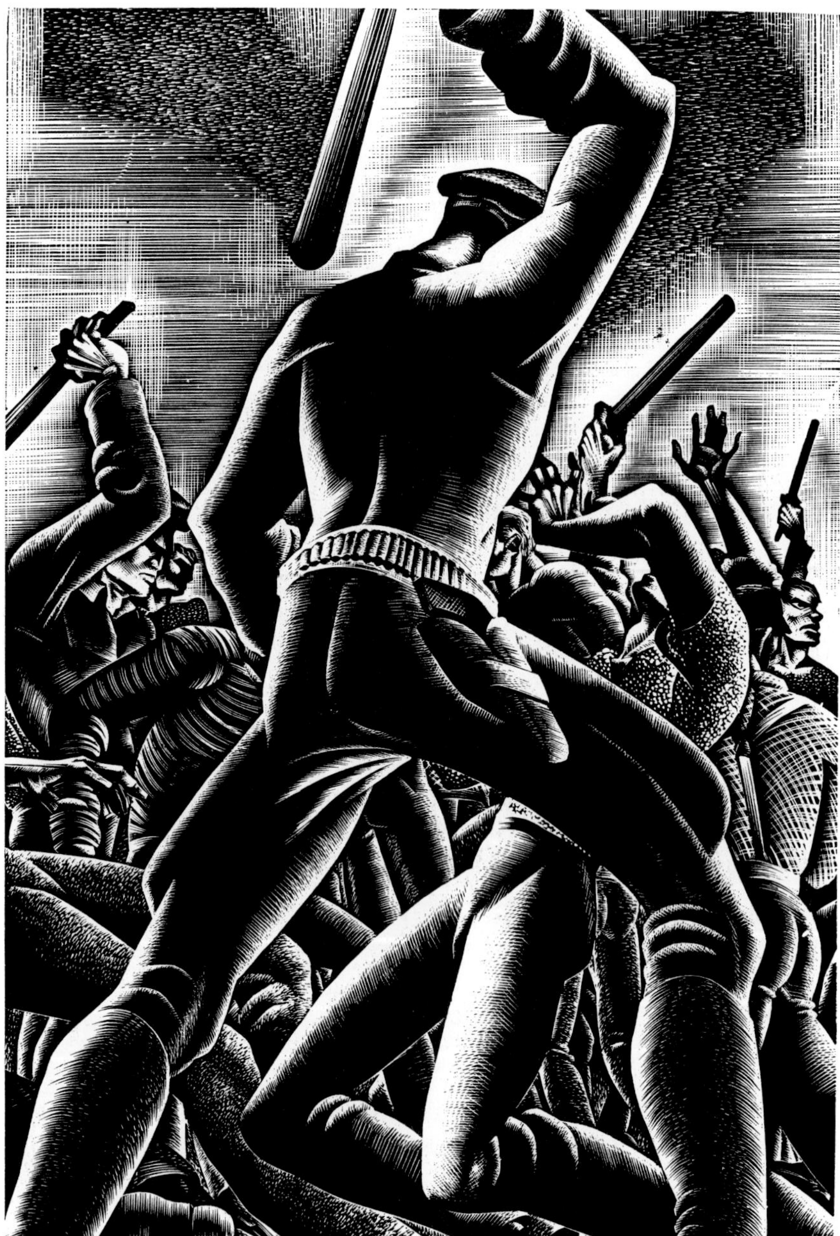

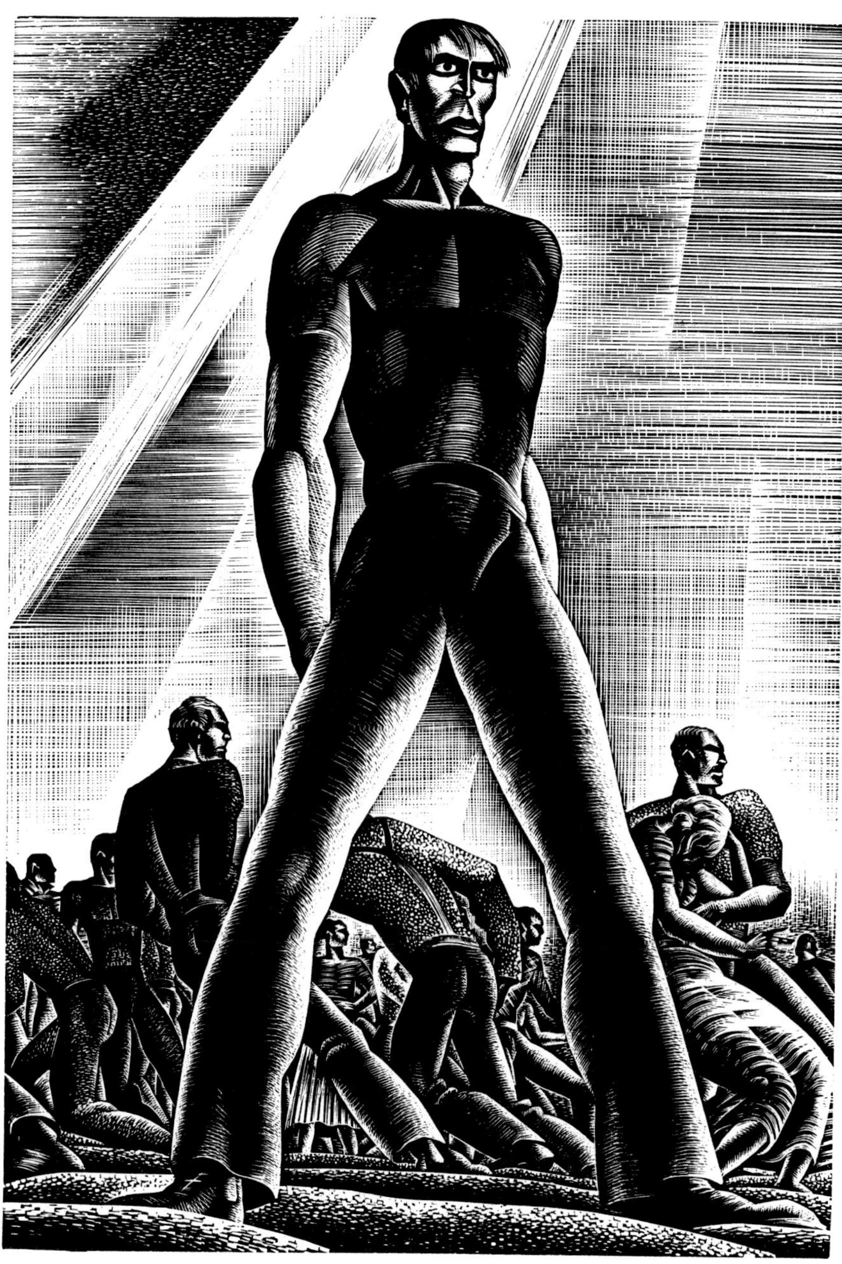

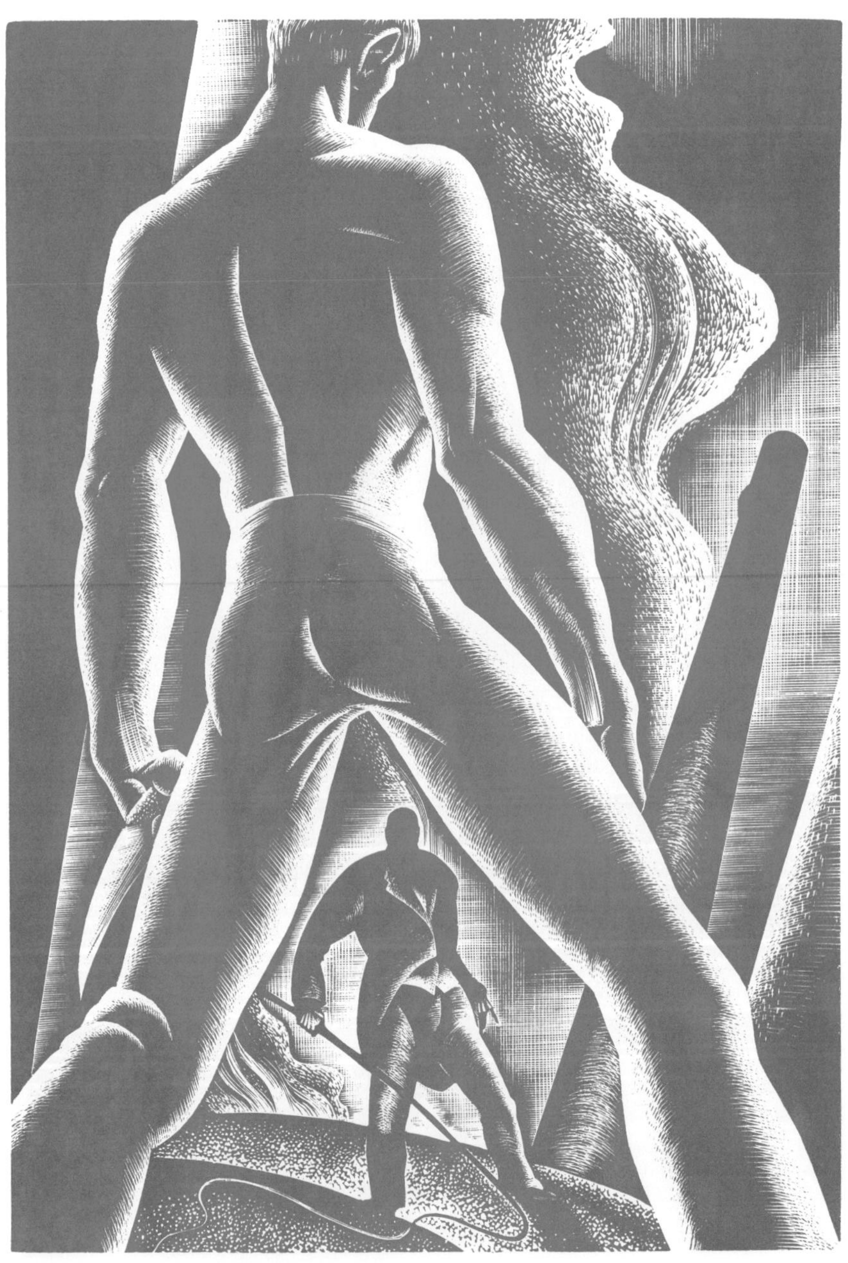

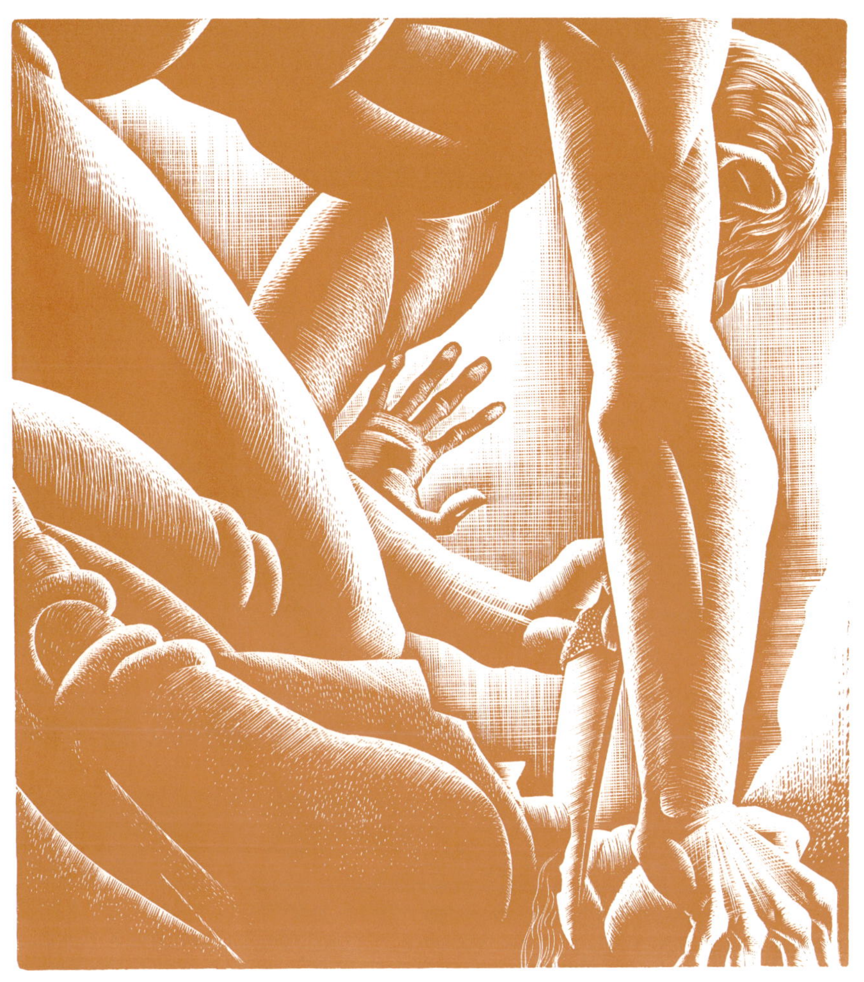

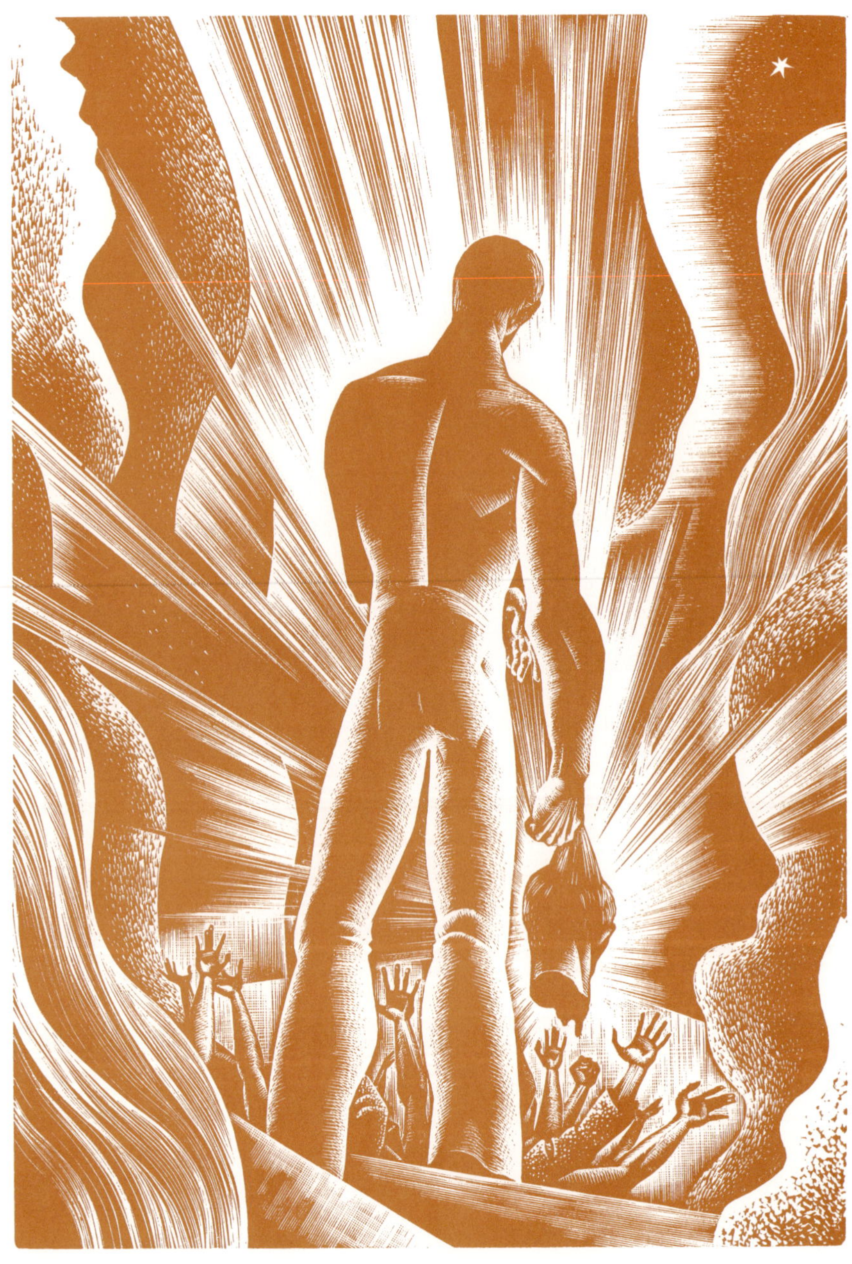

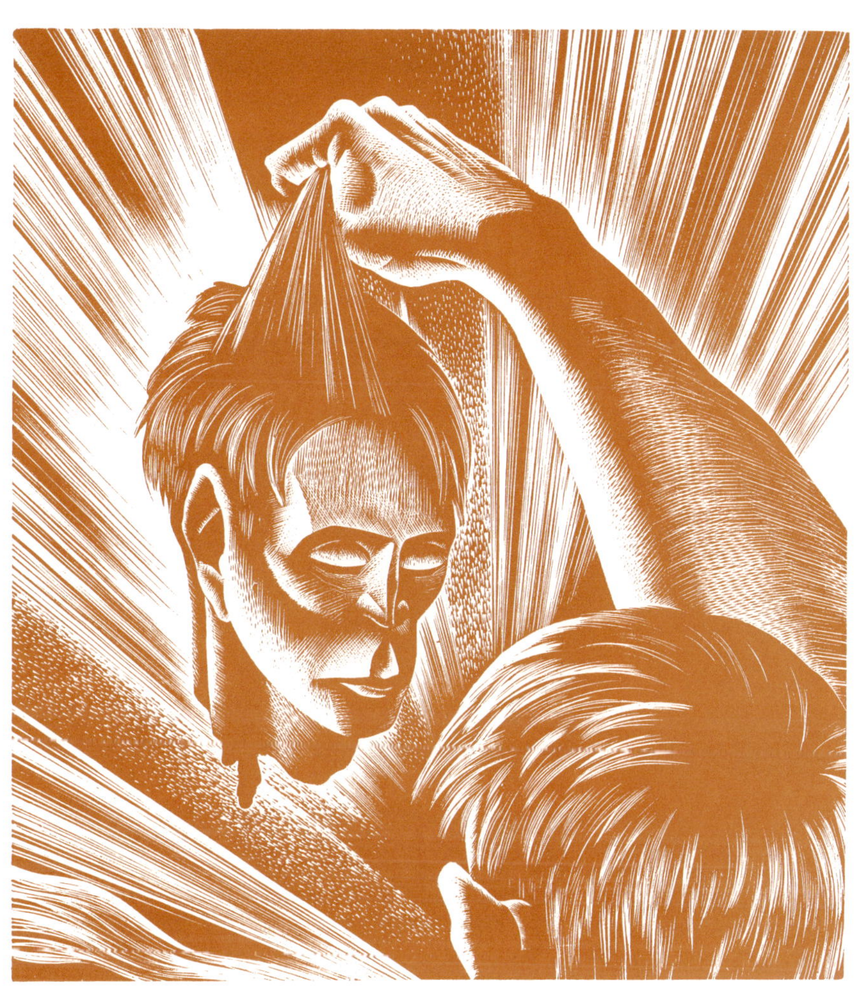

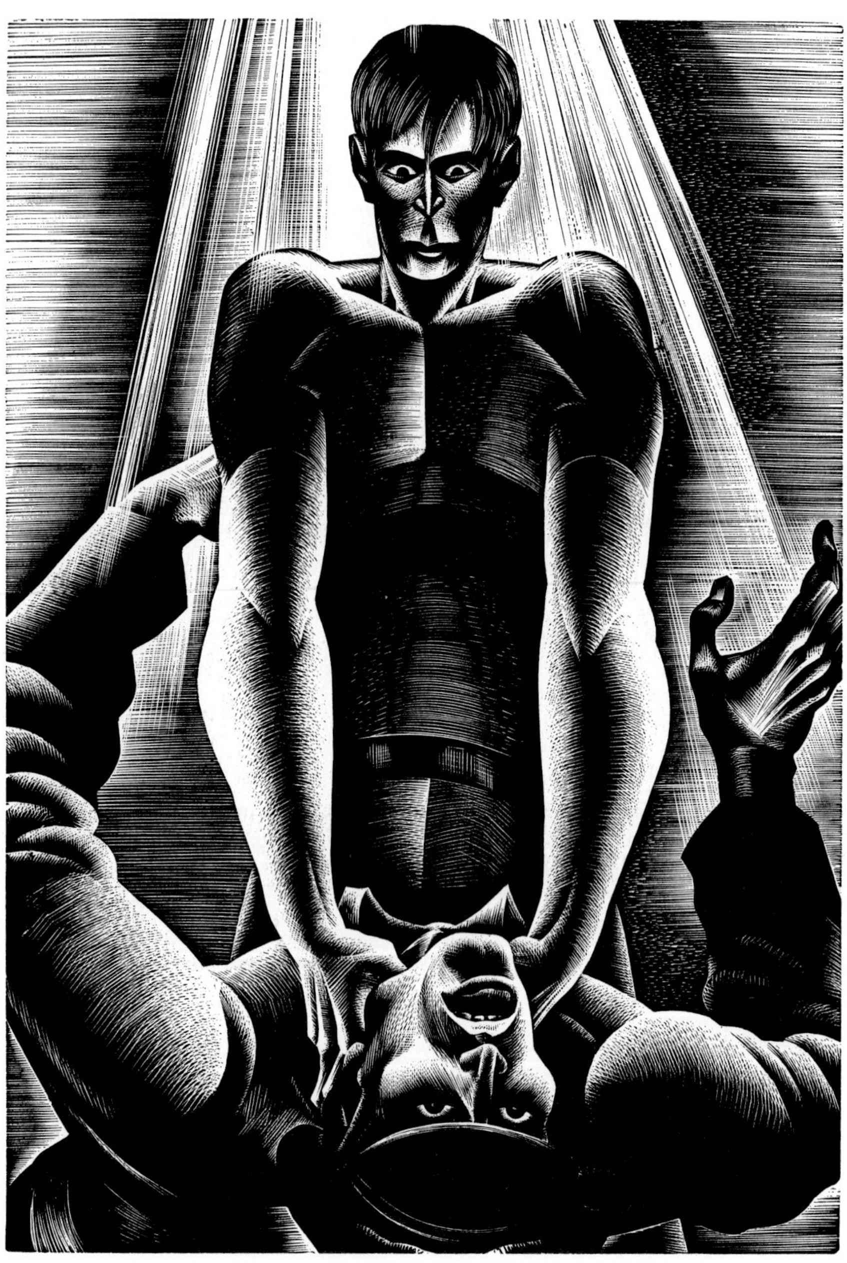

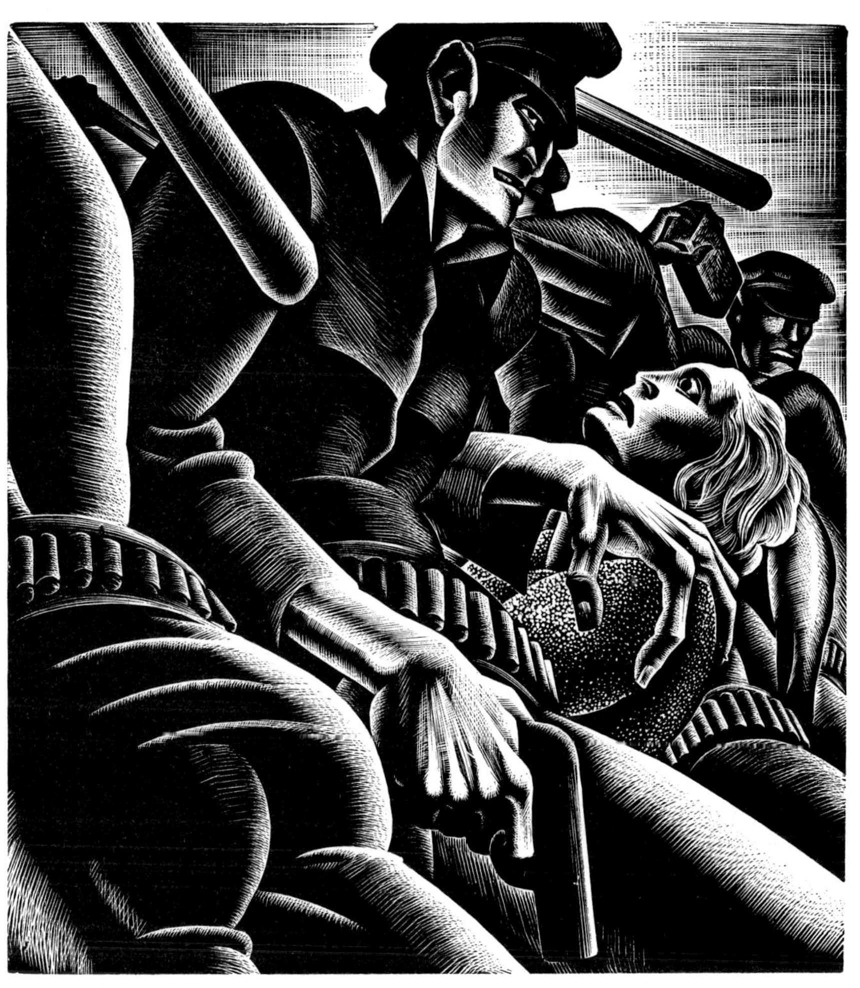

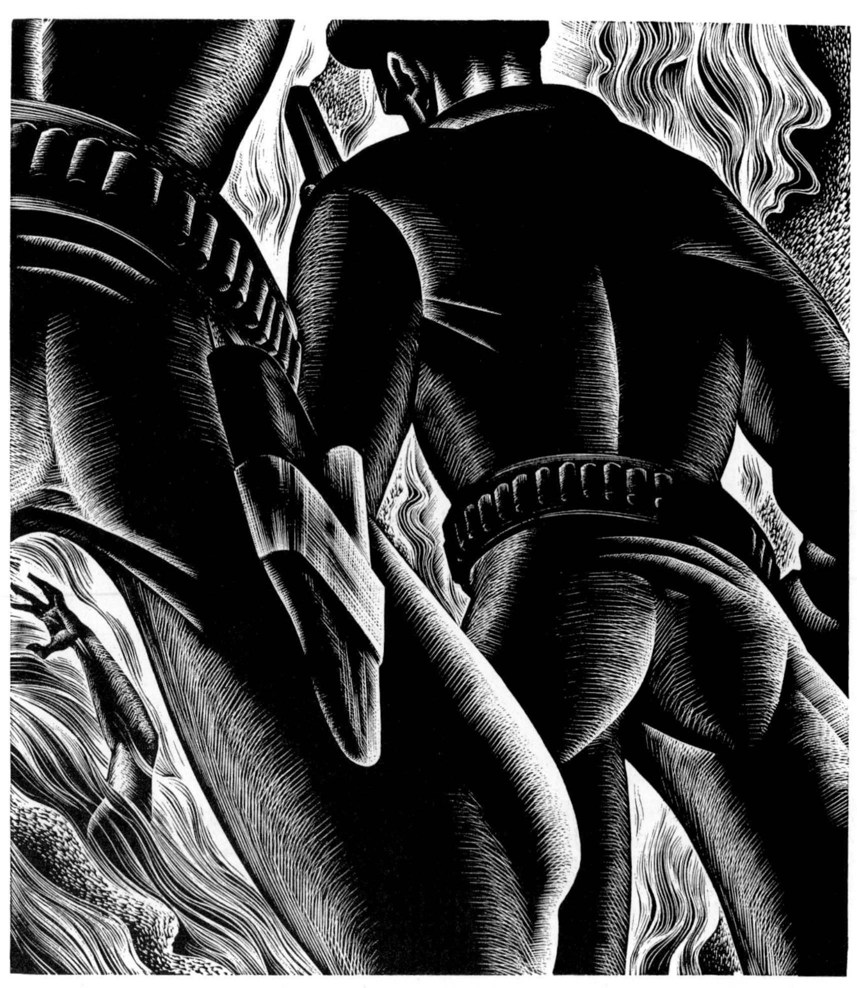

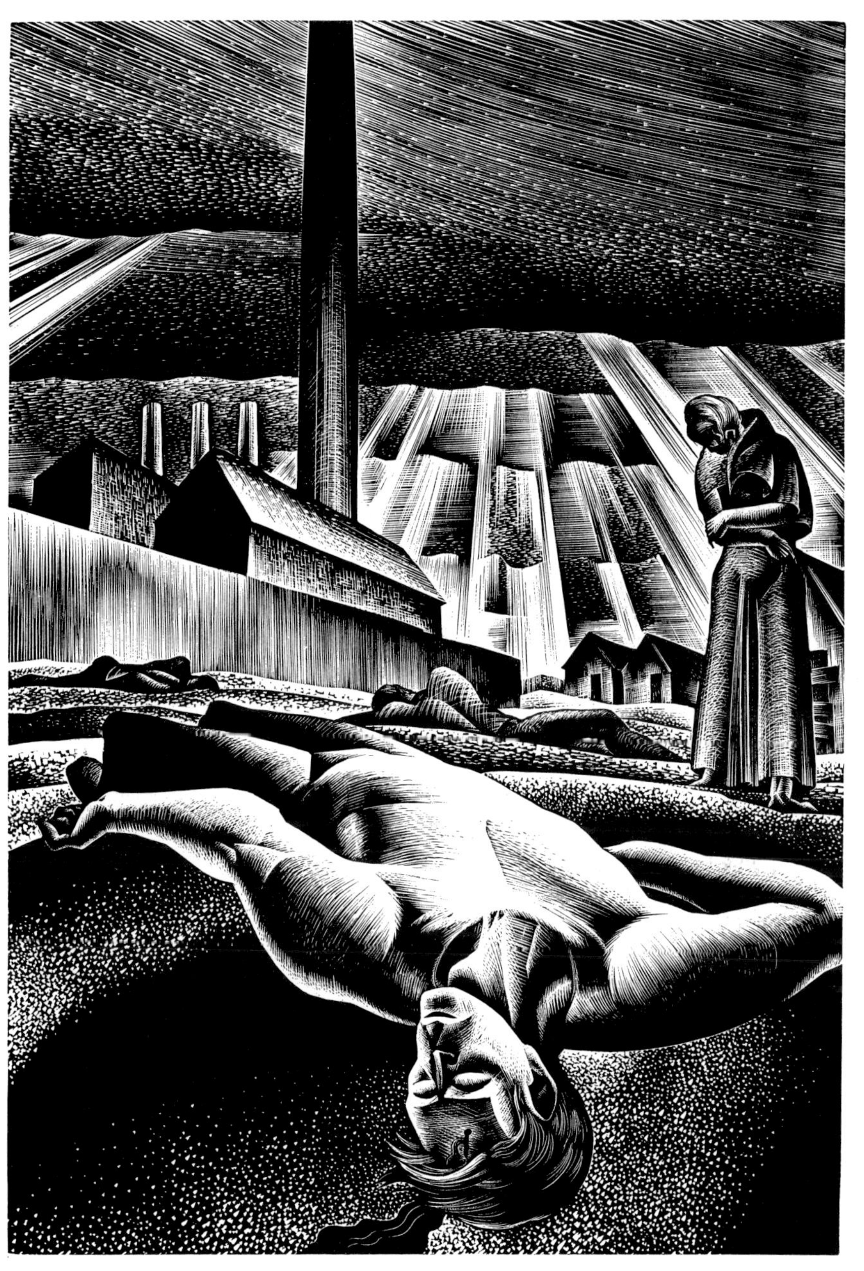

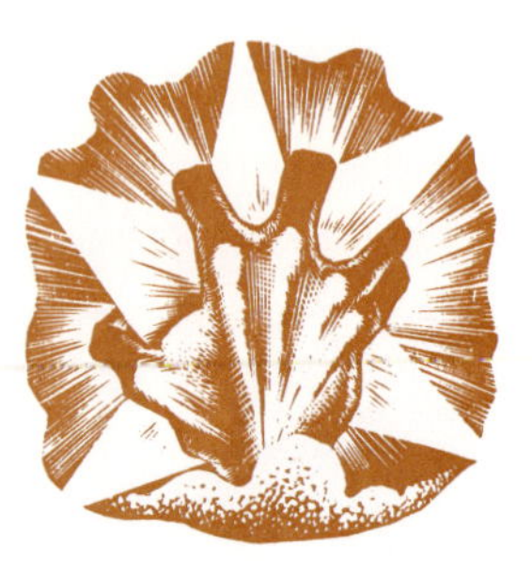